# SWING

# SWING

Lindsey Renée Backen

Ever Ink Press

admin@everinkpress.com

Editor: Jami Doddroe

Cover Photography: Sheila Backen

Publisher's Note: This is a work of fiction. Names, characters, places, and incidents are a product of the author's imagination. Locales and public names are sometimes used for atmospheric purposes. Any resemblance to actual people, living or dead, or to businesses, companies, events, institutions, or locales is completely coincidental.

For Grandma,
who taught me that anything is possible
with a bit of creativity. To Pop, who promised
to catch me until I learned how to fly.
I'm flying. I love you.

# 1

Trey Cunningham was the best dancer in Graceland. He secretly suspected that he might be the best in the whole county and maybe even the world. He stuffed his hands deeper into his pockets and stepped around a wad of gum on the sidewalk, glaring at his reflection in Mrs. Franklin's perfectly polished store window.

It was not skill that he lacked. It was height. He comforted himself with visions of the delayed growth spurt that would spur him into the ranks of the boys he avoided. Guys like Joe and Michael, who were showing off as they maneuvered Joe's blue Buick into a parking spot.

Trey ducked through the doors of the diner as the engine quieted in a temporary suspension from terrorizing the town. He was already late for work. He didn't have time to be caught on the sidewalk. Sliding the white apron over his head, he made a beeline to the soda fountain.

At the bar, Mrs. Jane Macy nibbled on fries, probably waiting for a glimpse of the widower Coplain. In the corner, Mr. Carter added a full basket of a burger and fries to his already bulging waistline. Jenny and Ruby giggled over malts, watching Joe and Michael walk past the window.

Trey studied each person, scoping for the one who was most

likely to lose a coin or two to the flashing jukebox in the corner. He wasn't allowed to play the music himself. Mr. Middleton didn't like the help starting the music, any more than Dave liked Trey wasting coins on something as fleeting as a song. The two giggling girls in the back gave him a glimmer of hope before he resigned himself to a potentially music-less workday.

No one was waiting for food, but Mrs. Maddie had apparently decided to leave the dishes for him to tackle. Trey stepped to the stainless-steel sink to dump the last of a float down the drain before plunging the glass into freshly drawn suds.

*Wash them like your life depends on it!* Mr. Middleton had repeated that phrase at least fifty times on Trey's first day of work. He dropped a stack of plates into the water, causing a small tsunami that threatened the welfare of his apron and clothing. In many ways, Trey's life did depend on it. Dave's veteran's compensation check wasn't going to cover the brothers' basic expenses this year, much less the holes wearing through the knees of Trey's jeans.

"Hey, shorty. How's it going?" Joe's voice irritated Trey even before he saw the slicked hair and square jaw that melted every girl in school.

*Be nice to the customer. Be nice to the customer. Be nice. Be nice. Be nice.*

Trey rubbed his apron. "You want the usual?"

"Yeah," Joe answered. He wadded a small piece of paper and flicked it across the counter. "I'm surprised you don't already have it waiting. Do we need to take you out back and retrain you?"

Trey winced, turning to plop a chunk of meat onto the stovetop. He could make a hamburger. He and Dave lived off them, but he didn't like preparing food. That was Mrs. Maddie's domain. Trey specialized in serving sodas and ice cream.

The Soda Shoppe was a good place to work, especially in the evenings when it became the local hangout. The girls dressed up. The boys brought their dates, and everyone hit the black and white tiles, dancing with the reckless enthusiasm of teens pent up in a small town.

It had been almost six years since the Cunningham Dance Studio closed, though it had been longer since it had actually made money. During the war, Trey's parents had opened the school for Friday night dances. It was their contribution to Uncle Sam, taking people's minds off the combat and their own thoughts off Dave.

"Hey, you! I wanted a Coke with that, eh?"

Trey jerked out of his memories, moving toward the soda fountain. He slid the soda in front of Joe, mumbling, "I was working on that."

"How about you get your head out of the clouds and pay attention?" Joe motioned toward Michael. "He's gotta eat too, you know."

"Yeah." Trey turned back toward the stove, flipping the first burger patty before adding another.

"What's the matter, Tracy?" Michael asked. "You fretting over starting the school year all alone?"

"It's Trey," he muttered.

"Poor little Tracy's got nobody to dance with. Maybe you could ask one of the elementary girls," Joe suggested. "They'd be just your size."

Trey glared at the browning patties, imagining throwing them against Joe's face and causing every girl in the place to swoon. He needed this job. He *needed* this job. Besides, he loved this job. If it weren't for these guys, it would be great.

He slapped butter onto the hamburger buns, toasting them on the grill before adding the meat. Just meat and cheese like the guys liked it. It didn't bother him. They'd smother them with so much ketchup that they wouldn't be able to taste the thing anyway. He added two sides of fries, jabbed toothpicks through the bun, and slid them to the boys. "Anything else?"

Joe shook the ketchup bottle. Trey took their silence as a "no" and stepped back to the dishes.

"Hey, Tracy!" Michael's voice held a twinge of mischief. "You're out of napkins." He tapped the metal box, echoing empty clinks.

Trey nodded, feeling tiny hairs prick on the back of his neck. "Now. We *need* them."

Trey allowed himself to roll his eyes toward the back wall before he used the toe of his shoe to scoot out a short stool from beneath the sink, wincing at the snickers behind him. The laughter grew as he stood on his toes to reach the box.

It was better than the first time he'd tried when he had to jump to even touch the top shelf. He had hoped the stool would make it less degrading, but when all was said and done, it was still humiliating. He cleared his throat, avoiding eye contact as he refilled the napkin holder.

Behind the boys, Mrs. Macy shuffled to the jukebox and punched in a number, sending a wink toward him. She knew he worked better with music. He resisted a smile as she gathered up her cane and hobbled through the door. It was strange to have an old lady flirt with him, but as long as she was providing music he didn't really care. His foot began to tap despite the two seniors at the bar.

By the time the boys had left, he was able to serve ice cream to Jane without resenting that she had brought Peter along. Peter, of all people to date. Peter was probably the worst dancer in the entire school, but he easily exceeded Jane's height requirement for a boyfriend.

Jane had been Trey's partner back in the first grade. They remained paired all the way up to middle school when she'd hit her growth spurt and he had stayed shorter than every girl in his class. Nothing improved in high school because the girls started wearing those stupid heels.

As the diner emptied, Trey added a few spins to his cleaning routine until the daylight faded outside. The dinner crowd abandoned the building as it filled with the teenagers of Graceland.

Trey ran his rag over clean tables as he eyed potential girls. He wasn't asking for a date, just a dance. Heck, he'd danced with every girl here at one time or another. The fact that he was an inch or two—or four—shorter than them had no effect whatsoever on his dancing skills.

When Julia's eyes flickered toward him and stayed a moment too long, he began working his way slowly toward where she stood in the corner with her friends. It would be easier if she'd go somewhere alone. Asking was hard enough without two other pairs of eyes watching him as he breathlessly waited for an answer.

When he inched too close, Julia led her posse to the far side of the room. Trey gave the last table a flourish to demonstrate his reason for being in that area and headed back to the safety of the counter.

Changing his focus, he waited until Jessica was alone before he leaned casually against the stool. "Hey, Jess. Wanna go for a spin?"

"I would, but I'm meeting Mark." Twirling her hair, Jessica flashed a dismissive I'm-sorry-but-not-really smile.

"Oh. Okay." Who was he to compete with Mark? He shrugged a shoulder. "Well, if you get bored later." He left his offer dangling and snatched up an empty glass to return to the sink. Jessica wasn't the only girl in the place. She would have danced with him if she hadn't already had a date. She was a one-man-at-a-time sort of girl.

Another round of cleaning and malt-making came and went before he zeroed in on Valerie, who leaned against the jukebox, ignoring every boy around her. She was known for not going steady, but she was worth a shot.

"How are you doing, Val?"

"I'm fine." Valerie kept her eyes down, flipping through the menu on the jukebox.

Trey peered past her shoulder. "Are you looking for a song in particular?"

"Not really."

"Oh." He tapped his fingers on the flashy top. "Well, if you think of a song, I can probably give you the number. I've got them all memorized."

"I'm just browsing."

Trey stepped back. "Okay. Well, when you find one, would you like to dance? My shift ends in about five minutes."

"Mmm." She scrunched her nose. "I'm more of a wallflower."

Trey's eyes swept over the dancers. "Me too."

A wilting wallflower. He left Valerie to her perusing, giving up for the night. A guy could only be turned down so many times. His ego was resilient, but it wasn't shatterproof.

Neither was his foot, he realized, as it caught the stool he'd forgotten to push back under the sink and sent him sprawling across the floor. He did a push-up to regain his feet. Just go with it. Hopefully, no one noticed.

But Olivia was sitting at the bar, sipping a Dr. Pepper. She wagged her eyebrows at him. "And he shall be called 'Grace from Graceland.'"

Trey took a bow with a flourish.

Olivia peered over the edge. "What's a stool doing back there anyway?" she asked.

"Um." He shoved it under the sink with his heel. "I dunno. It should be in the storage closet."

He glanced to the empty chairs on her left and right, wondering if he should risk it. Olivia was a pretty girl, though one couldn't get away with looking too idiotic in front of her before her remarks only added to the feeling of stupidity.

He glanced at the clock. He got off work early today. If he didn't find a partner before then, he'd have to go home without dancing. He couldn't stand around all night looking pathetic while everyone had a good time. He asked, "Are you alone tonight?"

"Nope." She sipped from the straw.

"Oh." He leaned against the counter. "Who are you with?"

"Mark."

"Ah." The infamous Mark. He nodded, pulling the white cap off his head along with the dumb apron. He glanced at Anna but couldn't find the heart to be turned down again. "Funny." His reply was sharp and pointed. "Jess is with Mark, too."

He hung up his things and saluted lightly on his way out, well aware that a small group of girls formed after his exit. Great. Now they'd talk about him. When he was safely around the block, he allowed his hands to seek comfort in his pockets. What was he doing wrong? Mark couldn't date every girl in that room.

He kicked up the stand to his bike and pedaled past the post office, his dad's old workplace, and finally his parents' abandoned studio. Mailboxes and fence posts flew by as Trey pumped the bike as fast as he could manage. He turned from the asphalt onto a dirt road that led to the white farmhouse.

Flies buzzed around the trash heap near the front porch as

Trey dumped his bike and jogged up the steps next to Dave's ramp. He had built that ramp himself when he was thirteen. You could tell, too. Dave's wheelchair gave a rush ride down, and he was unable to roll up again without help. Trey really should try to fix it to be a kinder slope.

He would, he thought, if Dave ever actually left the house. He yanked open the screen, kicking the base where the wood was beginning to rot from the last hundred times he'd gotten home.

"Hey, Dave, where are you?" he called.

"In the kitchen," Dave answered.

Trey flopped onto the couch to loosen his shoelaces. There was no reason to wear out his sneakers at home. He'd sworn to Dave that they would last, back when he was coaxing his brother to let him save for dancing shoes. He had counted on his feet growing, but—like the rest of his body—they had forgotten that turning into a teenager usually involved gaining a few inches.

He wanted those dancing shoes, so he had to make these last. He found his brother at the kitchen table, replacing the case of a radio while a second victim lay gutted nearby.

"How was your day?" Trey asked.

Dave grunted.

"Yeah." Trey dropped the wrapped hamburgers between the scattered knobs and screws. "Mine wasn't so great either."

Dave grunted again.

Trey moved to the sink to wash his hands. "Did you get the radio working?"

"Almost."

Trey dried his hands, then spun the towel a few times before launching it onto the counter by the dishes from last night. He dropped into the seat, pulling the repaired radio toward him. The box crackled and died.

Trey quirked his eyebrows. "Almost working, huh?"

Dave shrugged, unwrapping his burger. "It worked better before I slammed it against the table."

Trey whistled, shoving the device away. "Must have been quite the day."

He picked small holes in the top burger bun. He was sick of looking at burgers. He didn't want to eat another. Dave probably didn't either, but the man chewed like he'd never had one before. Trey peeked around for other damage, but Dave's temper must have been appeased by the destruction of the radio.

"I came up with a new dance move," Trey said. "You want to see it?"

"Sure."

Dave's consent came so unenthusiastically that Trey didn't bother showing it off. It wasn't terribly impressive to scoot across the floor alone. His finger traced the circling path of a tiny screw.

"Did you get any mail?" he asked.

"Nope."

Trey eyed his brother. None of the boy's war buddies would recognize him now. Even crippled, Dave had returned home with defined muscles. His arms were still strong from lifting all of his weight to move himself to and from the chair, but everything else had gone downhill.

The eyes that once charmed every girl in town had faded into a dull blue, like Trey's old toy airplane sitting under a layer of dust. Dave might still be handsome if he had a good trim and his jaw wasn't covered with a thick beard that made him look older than twenty-four. His hair was a shade darker than Trey's copper color.

He looked like their dad, only far older. Dave had been through hell fighting in the war, while Mr. Cunningham did his patriotic duty teaching people to dance back on the home front. Trey's eyes fell to the table. When Dave enlisted, he'd watched the news clips at the picture show and listened to the radio every day, determined to be a hero like his brother. But now, seeing Dave's health shattered by the war, he was glad he'd been too young to fight.

Dave's veteran's checks and side radio-fixing job might cover expenses if they weren't trying to keep their parents' home. Trey wanted to stay where his memories and childhood were created. Dave stayed because losing the farm meant moving into town, and moving into town meant that he'd be forced closer to people. People were the last thing Dave wanted to see, though sometimes Trey thought that was exactly what his brother needed.

"Why aren't you dancing tonight?" Dave asked.

Trey wadded his wrapping and tossed it into the brimming wastebasket. "I wanted to bring supper home for you."

Dave's eyebrows perched a bit higher.

Trey sighed. "I don't know, Dave." He snagged a glass and moved to the sink. "I don't know what's wrong. None of the girls will dance with me anymore. They all make up some stupid excuse about being with someone. They're not planning it either, because they all say it's the same guy."

"Maybe it is," Dave answered.

Trey's hand flailed, sending soap bubbles floating to the floor. "Mark wasn't even there. If they don't want to dance, why don't they just tell me they don't want to dance?" He spun toward his brother, shaking a sudsy finger. "One of these days, I'm going to hit that growth spurt, and then they're all going to be sorry."

One side of Dave's mouth cocked for the first time that day. "Because you're going to stop asking them to dance as soon as you get tall enough that they'll say yes?"

"No, but—" Trey stuttered. He glared at his brother's grin before turning back toward the sink. "Never mind."

"Golly, you're touchy."

Trey swallowed. "I've been turned down by three girls today."

Dave adjusted the wires in the back of the radio as he spoke. "There will always be women who are taller than you. You have your heart set on something that may or may not happen. You might stay short for your whole life."

"That doesn't mean I can't dance!" Trey plunged a cup into the water.

Dave turned his attention back to the radio. "Trash needs to be taken out."

Trey sighed and stooped to clean up the overflow, then stepped onto the porch.

"Not in your socks!" Dave echoed for their mother.

Trey peeled off his socks, creeping across the rough planks. He grumbled until he spotted a red car turning onto their lane. Dropping the bag to tumble down the steps alone, he rushed back inside. "Hey, Dave! Martha's coming."

Dave dropped the screwdriver and rolled himself away from the table. "Don't let her in."

"You could go out to the porch."

"No." The wheelchair swayed one way, then another. "Just tell her—send her away."

"Dave."

Already on his way to the bedroom, Dave threw Trey a glare that could kill a Nazi without the help of a bullet.

Trey growled and spun on his heels to grab the trash before any critters got into it.

Martha stood at the bottom of the porch steps, holding a covered pan. Her wheat-colored hair had been primly corralled into rolls beneath a dove-gray hat. Too much pink dusted her cheeks as she smiled at Trey. "Hi, Trey." Her voice held a slight tremble. "Is Dave here?"

Trey reached for the trash bag. "He's not feeling well."

Martha's smile flopped, replaced by concern. "Oh, dear. Is he sick?" She eyed him like a sage, reading secrets that weren't there. "Do you boys need a ride into town?"

"Um, no, he's just . . . you know. Not feeling good. He's tired."

Her shoes moved apart as she shifted to peer behind him. "Are you sure? Could I talk to him for a moment?"

Trey shifted to block her view, rubbing the back of his head. "Um. No, he's uh . . . he's asleep."

Something crashed in the living room. Trey managed a smile as the sleeping man swore.

"Oh, well." Martha's lips turned up as she took a step closer to the porch. "He's awake now."

"No." Desperate, Trey plastered himself between the woman and the house. He dropped his voice to a whisper. "You can't. It's not you, it's just . . . he's not *decent*."

That did it. Her cheeks reddened without the help of the rouge. "Oh." She backed off. "Oh, of course. I see. I'll—I see."

"Yeah." Trey scooted his foot across the porch, feeling tiny splinters scrape his toes.

Martha continued her retreat. "Okay, well, tell him I—I stopped by, and I hope he feels better." She thrust the pan into his hands. "Here, I made some extras. I thought you guys would enjoy them. Goodbye, Trey."

Her heels clicked away so quickly that Trey was afraid she might trip before she reached her car. Guilt gnawed, but it was too late to call her back to coax her into the home of an angry, ill-clad man. He tossed the trash into the burn pile with one hand and peeked under the cloth on his way back inside. "Hey, Dave. She brought you brownies!"

Despite the announcement, it was still a full minute before Dave rolled back into the living room. "What'd you tell her?"

"I told her you weren't wearing anything."

Dave's eyebrows flew up before he replied dryly, "Thanks, Trey. Thanks."

"Well, she might never come back. That's what you wanted, isn't it?" Trey dug out a square with his fingers, tasting chocolate and sugar and butter. "I hope she does, though. These are good."

Dave didn't touch the brownies. He spent the evening dismantling the radio again until they couldn't see by the sunlight anymore. Sometime in the last few months, Dave had decided that using lights, even at night, was a waste of electricity.

When the house was dusky, Dave used his arms to lift himself from the chair to his bed, but Trey had to help remove the shoes and jeans from the useless legs. He tried not to look, and he tried not to shudder. Sometimes he dreamed he woke to find himself crippled like Dave. It wasn't an irrational fear. It could happen to anyone. It had happened to Dave.

Dave had danced. He'd played football. He'd ridden horses. He'd run over communist territory until, suddenly, it was all gone. He couldn't even move his legs without using his arms.

Dave panted as he pulled the covers over himself. Then he gave Trey the bland smile that was an unspoken thank you. "Night, kid."

# 2

Trey had brownies for breakfast on his way to work. He'd left Dave awake, dressed, and settled in his chair, still working on Mrs. Miller's radio. He hadn't told Dave that Mrs. Miller had already bought a new one. The truth was that Dave wasn't very good at fixing radios, but he couldn't do the things he once excelled in, so people kept asking him for minor repairs.

It hadn't been so bad at first, living on their own. Their parents had money in savings on top of Dave's compensation check. Dave had found work when he first returned, but between his disability and worsening temper, even the most patient employer eventually let him go. Now he simply didn't try.

Trey couldn't resent it. Dave had given up his life for his country. Who was he to begrudge working on a Saturday at a job he would have regardless of whether his brother could walk or not? He let himself into the diner, eyeing the jukebox.

Mrs. Maddie's voice floated from the back, cutting off his cheerful greeting. "But Betty, Trey needs this job. You know that. He might chat a little more than he should, but he gets everything finished. I think it's admirable of him, the way he takes care of his brother."

"I think his brother needs to find his spine." Betty must be delivering the bread. He heard a thud like she'd dropped a crate. "Do you know Martha went to see him, and he wouldn't even come out of the house?"

"Really?"

"Yes. She wouldn't say why. She just said he wouldn't, and the poor girl looked like she was going to cry. I don't know why she keeps going over there."

"Oh, you know Martha's liked him since they were little things."

Trey swallowed and went back to the door, opening and shutting it hard enough to make it jingle. Mrs. Maddie hurried from the kitchen, wiping her hands on her apron, and greeting him rather loudly. "Trey!"

"Morning!" Trey flashed her a smile.

The back door shut as Betty let herself out. Mrs. Maddie busied herself cracking eggs at the stove. "Flip that sign, will you? We were just opening. You sure didn't stay long after work last night."

Trey ducked his head, pretending it was to put on his apron. "Nah." He would normally say he went home for Dave, but after that conversation, he didn't dare mention his brother.

Maddie planted a hand on her hip, cocking her head. "Are you all right?"

"Yeah, I'm fine." He sent her a half-hearted smile before turning his attention to rolling the silverware. If people were complaining about him, he had to combat the rumor mill. He couldn't start losing jobs like Dave. Besides, out of all the places in town, he wanted to work here.

"Is it because no one would dance with you last night?" Mrs. Maddie asked.

Trey flinched. "Nah, it's cool."

She set her hand on his arm. "Don't you worry. Somewhere there's a girl for you. You'll find her." She nodded until her earrings jingled.

Sheriff Morgan came in for the first breakfast plate, sparing Trey from a reply. The morning rush eased the ache as he exchanged coffee for tidbits of gossip.

He was scrubbing the breakfast dishes, getting ready to start lunch, when Mrs. Maddie seized his arm, making him drop the plate and slosh water onto his clothes. "Trey, look."

Trey glanced toward where she was not so subtly bobbing her chin. The bell on the door tinkled as a girl stepped inside the diner.

It wasn't the red, polka-dotted dress that caught Trey's attention. It wasn't the jarring way that they clashed with her gray shoes. It wasn't even how her hair fell over her shoulder in brown strands that shimmered in the sunlight, or how her eyes looked like melted chocolate, or even that she walked straight toward the jukebox.

What caught Trey's attention was the fact that her head was even with the top of jukebox. His heart did a funny little flip-flopping dance as Mrs. Maddie shoved him to the counter before disappearing into the kitchen. He reached for a rag, swiping the clean surface while he rearranged panic into cool indifference.

There were only three people in the diner to witness his fate. Mr. Morris ate at the far side of the bar, squinting at his plate like he thought there might be a bug hiding in the food. Susan was eating with Neil Smith at a booth talking about the latest additions to the library.

The girl circled the diner slowly, hugging herself, taking far too much interest in the pictures on the wall. Was she working up the nerve to come talk to him?

Mr. Morris shoved his plate away, dropped a nickel for a tip, and hobbled toward the exit, where he tried to push through the glass window.

Trey rushed to take the elderly man's arm to guide him toward the exit. "Wrong panel, Mr. Morris. The door is here."

Mr. Morris grinned with gapped teeth. "Oh! It's there, you say. Well, I suppose you'd know better than me."

Once Trey had guided the man safely through the exit, he turned to find the girl cocking one eyebrow with half a grin on her face. He shrugged lightly at her before heading back to the bar where he busied himself making a Coke float. He'd talk to her, by golly, if it took him all day.

He hesitated, then blurted, "Are you just passing through town?"

She spun on one foot, meandering toward the counter. "I won't be here long."

Trey motioned toward the glass. "Well, we had someone order a Coke float, but they had to leave. It hasn't been touched if you'd like it."

She eyed the glass. "Your boss won't get mad?"

"Nah." He kept his voice light. "We don't get many visitors in Graceland."

"Yeah, I noticed." There was a slight, overwhelmed laugh in her answer.

Trey nudged the float closer to tempt her. "So? It's melting."

The corners of her lips perked before her chin rose. "I like root beer."

"I can do that." He drew out the "I" and spun to make a generous float, glad the place was almost empty.

He glided it in front of her and snagged the Coke. "Guess that leaves me to drink the extra."

"I guess so." She rolled her eyes, but it was accompanied by a smile.

Trey leaned on the counter and helped himself to the Coke. "I'm Trey."

She nodded and sipped on the straw, offering no name in reply.

He grinned. "And you are . . . Mary?"

She shook her head.

Trey cocked an eyebrow. "Jane, Susan, Linda?"

Her eyes sparkled. "Not even close."

Trey pursed his lips. "Come on, help me out."

"You'll never guess it."

"Give me a clue?"

She ran the spoon through her lips. "That was the clue."

"Cynthia? Sharon?"

"Nope." She jabbed the spoon back into her ice cream.

Trey stared. Why were girls so complicated? "You're really not going to tell me?"

"Nope."

"So, how long will you be in Graceland?"

"Not long."

"Oh." His heart tumbled. "Longer than today?"

"Probably."

He arched a brow. "'Probably' meaning what?"

"'Probably' meaning as little time as possible."

"Oh." Well, shoot. Trey stirred the float with his straw. "It's not a bad place when you get to know it. You should come here tonight. All the teenagers have a big dance." His eyes flickered to hers. "Do you dance?"

She folded two dainty hands under her chin. "Do you?"

Trey's insides warmed as he rested his forearms on the counter. "I can do just about every dance that exists. If you come tonight, I could show you a few steps."

She waited a moment before answering, "I might."

"So what kind—"

The door gave harsh clinks in place of its friendly chime. Reverend Howard's black, glossy shoes had never stepped into the Soda Shoppe. Their owner's mouth drew into a tight line as he zeroed in on the kids. "Lila, I told you to wait in the car." His smile didn't cover the suppressed irritation that laced his pleasant tone.

Lila dropped her head back to look up at the man. "I know."

"Then why are you here?"

"You took too long. I got hot."

Reverend Howard sent a pinning glare toward Trey as though suspecting that the boy had gone out to the car and coaxed the girl inside. "When I tell you to do something, I expect you to obey."

"This is Trey." The girl ignored the man's order as she gestured toward Trey. "It's rude of me not to introduce you."

"Yes, I know Trey," Reverend Howard said. "His family attended our church a long time ago."

"Oh, yeah. Um . . ." Trey scooted his ice cream glass across the inch between his hands. "We haven't been in a while."

"Perhaps you ought to return. God doesn't want His children to hide from Him." Reverend Howard offered a hand to the girl, which she ignored as she slid off the stool. "I don't want you coming in here anymore." He moved suspicious eyes toward Trey. "We don't dance. Come along, Lila."

With that disappointing announcement, he marched her toward the door.

"Goodbye, Lila." Trey grinned as he tested her name. Lila.

Lila and Trey. Trey and Lila. They went well together, like a dance team. He picked up the two glasses and carried them to the sink before the kitchen door swung open, nearly knocking him in the nose. He should have known Mrs. Maddie had been peeking through the cracks.

"Who is she? And what was he doing here?"

"She's Lila, and he's hosting her, I guess."

Mrs. Maddie's hands fisted on her hips as her lips pulled together. "Well, I'll be a—mmmmmmm . . ." Her eyes sparkled as she shook a finger in the air, pacing a few steps. "Wait a minute." She spun back toward him. "I bet I know who that girl is! She's about your age, right?"

Trey waited for an explanation, but Mrs. Maddie just smiled to herself and turned back to the stove.

"What?" Trey pressed closer. "Who is she?"

"I'll bet she's his granddaughter."

Trey blinked. "Reverend Howard has kids?"

"A daughter. He did. I knew her. Pretty little thing she was."

"What happened to her?"

She cocked an eyebrow. "Her name was Ruth, and she was always a troubled child. Oh, she was nice enough, but he held her too tightly. Poor thing couldn't even breathe without him telling her she was doing it wrong. She disappeared one day. Just disappeared like that." She snapped. "There were some new guys in town at the time, coming in to work the harvest, but they didn't stay long. I'll bet you anything that girl had something to do with it. Now she's here, but not Ruth. Oh, I wonder!"

She looked sad and upset and excited and brimming with juicy news all at the same time. If Trey never got to speak to the girl again, he'd still hear all about her from Mrs. Maddie.

Despite his excitement, his thoughts crept around the condemning words. *We don't dance.*

She had to dance. She was perfect.

Twenty minutes later, Mrs. Melba bustled through the door and perched on one of the same stools she normally accused of being an endangerment to her health.

Today, she wobbled with courage, risking life and limb as she leaned across the counter to hiss, "Maddie, you will never guess! I've just heard it from Samuel. Reverend Howard has a girl with him, and she's Ruth's daughter!" She shook her finger. "What did I tell you? What did I tell you? She was pregnant when she left!" Her voice dropped to a whisper. "Who do you think the father is?"

Mrs. Maddie glanced around the diner before huddling close. "I don't know. Who?"

Mrs. Melba pulled back. "I don't know. That's why I'm asking you."

"Remember that quiet guy she hung out with?" Mrs. Maddie asked. "What was his name?? I don't think I ever heard him say a word the entire month he was here." She gripped Trey's arm like they were comrades in a conspiracy. "You must find out, Trey. School starts Monday. She'll probably be in your class."

"Yes!" Mrs. Melba turned eager eyes onto him. "My goodness. Yes, she would be about your age. Well, that cancels out your father. He was married before she left." She spoke through the side of her mouth toward Martha. "That's probably why she left."

Trey choked. "What?"

"Oh, well, he dated Ruth a while." Mrs. Maddie pawed the air as though it didn't matter. "They were never serious. When he met your mama, well, he was gone. I never saw a man fall so hard so fast."

"Really, Trey," Mrs. Melba said. "Find out and ask what happened to her mama."

Great. Now he was being used as a spy.

Trey hesitated. "I don't think—"

"Oh, I'm going to church tomorrow," Mrs. Melba said. "I'll find out."

Mrs. Maddie set down her rag. "Melba, you're not Methodist!"

"I know, but every year we work with the Methodists for the annual food drive." Melba's eyes opened wider. "*I'm* not prejudiced."

"You've never been to a Methodist service!"

"Well, there's no reason not to pop over there. Ruth was a dear friend, you know." Her eyes lit. "Oh, perhaps she'll be there!"

"No. No, that girl was alone." Mrs. Melba shook her head.

"Pity, really. You don't think Reverend Howard intends to raise her, do you? That man's got no business raising children."

"Oh, she seems spirited enough. She'll survive," Mrs. Maddie replied. "She looks a lot like Ruth, doesn't she?"

"Don't you worry. I'll get the whole story." Mrs. Melba tapped long fingernails against the counter. "Oh, I'm just dying of curiosity."

By this time, Trey was too, though he fought to sound casual as he asked, "Do you think she'll stay?"

"I imagine." Mrs. Melba's chin jerked toward him. "Now, don't you be getting your sights set on her. She could be the nicest girl in the world, but there's no way the reverend will let you get near her. Ruth wasn't allowed to dance."

"Well, maybe I could talk to him."

The woman laughed and patted his hand. "Poor boy. No, I'm afraid you'll never dance with Ruth's daughter."

Early the next morning, however, Trey adjusted one of Dave's dusty ties around his neck and tamed his hair with gel. He wasn't sure how to explain his choice of Sunday attire to his brother, so he surmised that the man was too tired to wake and should rest until noon today. He was careful not to slam any doors during his exit.

By the time he biked into town, his clothes were more wrinkled than they had been when he dug them from the pile on his closet floor. He found a bush and hid his bike, then strode toward the church. He had a right to be here. He'd been here every Sunday as a kid. Even so, he lingered in front of his parents' graves, working up the nerve to go inside.

A little gray dress that now matched the dull shoes caught his attention, and he inched toward the front doors after Lila disappeared. There were no assigned pews in the church, and he intended to sit with her. He grimaced, watching Reverend Howard seat Lila in the second row from the front.

As soon as the man turned his back, Trey slipped to the pew, wondering at the change in Lila's attire. Yesterday she'd looked like a girl from 1951. Today, she looked like she was wearing her grandmother's old things.

"You never told me how long you were staying," Trey said as he plopped onto the pew.

Lila jumped, then smoothed her skirt against her legs without looking toward him. "I did tell you. I'm staying as little time as possible."

"You'll be at school tomorrow, right?"

"That's the plan." She squinted toward the lamb in the stained-glass window. "My grandmother's sick today, so who knows? Maybe I won't go."

Trey's heart thumped as he made himself at home on the pew. "You're in the tenth grade?"

"Yes."

"So am I. We'll have all the same classes."

"Oh."

Trey frowned, confused by her replies. "You didn't come last night," he said.

Lila shrugged. "I was in prison."

Trey laughed. "Yeah. I guess that's pretty close to the truth. How is life with your grandfather?"

Lila glanced at her clothing. "I think his mind was left in the last century."

"Trey?" Reverend Howard interrupted the conversation. "It's good to see you in church."

"Yes, sir." Trey jumped to his feet, almost stuttering. "I stopped by to see my parents. Their graves, I mean. I decided maybe it was time to be coming back."

"Hmm." The man's nose stayed level with the ground, but his eyes swooped down on the pair. "It's good to see you've become concerned about your eternal future. So many youths these days think themselves invincible."

Trey's face pricked. "Yes, sir."

"Perhaps you'd like to sit with the Millers? They have plenty of room in their pew."

Trey glanced at the couple. Mr. Miller blew into a handkerchief. His wife's head hung in a doze before the service even started.

If Trey were any other boy in town, he would reply that his current row had even more space and refuse to budge, but he wasn't any other boy. He was Trey. The only thing he could think to say was, "Yes, sir."

His exile was delayed by Mrs. Melba and Mrs. Thompson, who had set aside their feud over who had the best pie recipe and united in curiosity.

Before anyone could say anything, Reverend Howard gestured toward Lila with a smile. "This is my granddaughter, Lila."

"Oh, she's so beautiful," Mrs. Thompson crooned.

Mrs. Melba leaned closer to Lila, who responded by pressing back against the pew. "You look like your mama," the woman fished. "But I'll bet you've got some of your father in there, too, don't you?"

"Not a bit," Lila answered.

"Where are your parents now?"

Lila's eyes flickered for the smallest second toward her grandfather. "They're dead."

A stunned silence fell over the group, and even the murmurs in the nearby pews faded.

"Oh, I'm so sorry," Melba answered, sounding more excited than sorry. "How did it happen?"

"Well." Lila swallowed, wiggling as her eyes filled. "The Christmas that I turned ten, we lived in New York, and there was a terrible blizzard. When it stopped, my neighbors and I found my parents' car buried under a five-foot drift. They weren't inside, but we found two sets of tracks in the snow."

Mrs. Melba shuddered as though she was trapped in the snow herself.

"They'd run out of gas because of the rationing, so they'd continued on foot," Lila explained. "We found where Mama fell, and Daddy had picked her up. The snow was past my waist, but I could get through by following Daddy's tracks. You could see where he struggled. He must have walked for hours, trying to make it into town. We found them frozen in an embrace, and they buried them together, just like they died." Nearly the entire church was quiet as she finished the tragic tale.

The reverend wore a peculiar expression, but he only waved to break up the crowd. "We're starting service. Everyone, please find a seat."

Trey found a seat about six inches away from Lila. He was so close that he smelled her lavender soap. He hardly heard the sermon. She eyed him. He glanced at her. Once, she looked like she might laugh. The reverend glared from the pulpit, emphasizing the eternity of hell that awaited all sinners.

As soon as the last song ended and people began to chat, Lila grabbed Trey's hand and towed him toward the doors. As they reached the bottom of the steps, she turned to him. "You're persistent."

"I can be."

"What are you doing here?"

He shrugged. "I came here all the time when I was a kid."

"So it had nothing to do with me?"

He gave her a sheepish smile. "Maybe a little."

She tucked hair behind her ear, grinning as she turned to walk. "How come you stopped coming to church?"

"I stopped when my parents died."

"How'd they die?"

He was surprised she asked, though she'd just told him her own tragic tale without seeming too disturbed. "Dad flipped the car." Their deaths hadn't been romantic. He pointed toward the graveyard. "They're out there."

"At least you can talk to them," Lila replied, seeming comforted by the thought.

Trey glanced sideways. "They're dead."

"They can probably still hear you. Don't you believe they're in Heaven or somewhere?"

Trey shrugged. "I guess. I really don't know where they are."

"Me neither." She squinted against the sun. "I've never been to church before."

"Never?"

"I probably wasn't supposed to tell you. My grandfather

doesn't approve of the way I was raised and thinks he can erase it or something."

That sounded intriguing. "Why? How were you raised?"

"Oh . . ." Her voice took a light, nasty tone that confused him as to whether or not she was joking. "We were in the circus."

"The circus?"

She laughed, swinging lightly on the graveyard gate. "I'm joking. Where are you from?"

"Here."

"You grew up here?"

"Yeah."

"Where do you live?"

"On the edge of town. I biked in."

"You don't have a car?"

"Nope."

She seemed disappointed. "Too bad. I don't have one either." She walked down the ramp, kicking at the railing. "I guess you don't drive."

"I'm going to learn soon. We have a car. It's just not running yet."

"Good." She smiled. "I like you."

"I like you, too."

"So you're the new girl." Georgia stepped into the graveyard, followed by Betty. They eyed Lila as if she was a mouse.

"I guess," Lila replied. "I won't be here long."

"You're not going to school?" Betty asked.

"I might for a week or so."

"Well, you'll need to find a new dress and shoes," Georgia smirked. "What are you wearing? Old rations?"

Trey blushed for her, but Lila's eyebrows only cocked. "The reverend's rations," she answered. "He assured me this was the only proper church attire. Who knows? Maybe it is, and you're all going to hell for wearing those dresses."

Two sets of eyes widened, and one mouth fell open. Lila almost smirked before she spun on her gray flats.

Lila grabbed Trey's hand. "Come on. Let's go talk to your parents."

"Uh," Trey sputtered.

Lila towed him toward the graveyard as Betty's voice carried behind them. "She's joking, right?"

Lila's eyes sparkled as she glanced around the headstones. "Where are they?"

Trey pointed.

Lila dropped in front of his father's stone. "Hi. I brought your son. He's sorry he hasn't come sooner. He didn't know you could hear him." She glanced up at Trey. "Say 'hi.'"

"Uh," Trey said.

"Good enough for now."

"She's talking to the graves," Betty hissed.

"So how have you been, Mr. Cunningham?" Lila asked. She pressed her ear to the ground and nodded before looking at Trey. "He's fine."

Georgia planted her hands on her hip. "If you can really talk to him, ask him how he died."

"That seems rather rude," Lila said, but she looked back at the grass. "Did you hear her? She wants to know how you died." She listened gravely, nodding before she replied, "It was a car accident. He doesn't want to talk about it. What's that, Mr. Cunningham?" She cocked her head before swinging it toward Georgia. "He says to tell you Mr. Medders wants his wife's ring given back to her."

Georgia stiffened, then sputtered, "How'd you . . ." She planted her hands on her hips. "You don't know what you're talking about."

"No, not really. I'm just passing along the message." Lila's eyebrows rose at them until the girls backed out of the graveyard, leaving a trail of nasty names in their wake.

Trey blinked. "You sure know how to scare people off."

"Not well enough." Lila sighed as she stood, brushing off her palms and eyeing her shoes.

"What did you mean about Mr. Medders?"

"Georgia took Mrs. Medders' ring."

"How do you know?"

She shrugged. "A little bird on the party line."

A little bird sounded much better to Trey than thinking his deceased father was speaking to his future girlfriend. He took a step closer. "So, do you want to go for a walk? I could show you—"

"Lila!" The reverend's voice carried from the front in a tone that insisted on being answered at once. "Lila, we're going home."

Lila's eyes flashed with disappointment as she stepped toward the gate. "See you at school?"

"Yeah." Trey's hands found their homes in his pockets. "I have to get home anyway."

"Okay." She flashed a smile and darted for the churchyard.

School never looked so good.

# 3

Cracked fingers dug into broken slabs of the walkway. Dave dragged himself on his belly, ducking his head as debris collapsed around him. His legs lay useless, buried under a mound of concrete and twisted iron bars.

*Home.*

He'd never wanted to come here. Seven of his classmates had signed up and talked him into it. He couldn't be seen as a coward.

*Home.*

Tears and dirt mixed in his eyes, blinding him to bodies strewn around him. He just wanted to go home. He couldn't fight anymore with two shattered legs. He could get out of this hell. He had a little brother at home.

When Dave had last seen him, Trey had still been running as fast as his short legs could carry him, waving at the train as it picked up speed. A letter from the boy lay in his pocket right next to the perfume-scented note from Lucy. Lucy, who had given him his first kiss in secret behind the schoolhouse and his last in front of everyone at the station.

*Home.*

The rumbling ground warned of an incoming tank, loosening a second shower of debris. Civilians screamed as they rushed past him toward shelter. Someone stumbled over his head, kicking his helmet beyond reach.

He struggled to work his legs free of the demolished wall, crying in a way he would have once called cowardly. Pain rippled through his calves as something dug deeper into his flesh. Vehicles thundered through the streets, sending the last of humanity scurrying into the buildings. Soldiers jumped from the side of the trucks, kicking in doors and initiating another round of screams from inside as the bullets sprayed the walls.

He had to get home. It couldn't end here. Dave clawed and kicked, swimming in a sea of debris. He reached back, feeling broken fingernails shoot pain as he tried to scoop away the rubble. Kick. Get free. Go home.

A boot heel crushed his shoulder, pinning him against the ground. German words spat over his head.

"*No,*" he panted. He had to go home.

He raised his head to the blue eyes that peered out from a grim, sooty face as the barrel of a gun leveled toward him. "*No!*"

The man's finger tightened on the trigger, releasing the bullet as the ground rumbled again.

"No!"

His own shout woke him. Dave gasped for breath, fighting the sheets away from his torso while his legs continued their slumber at the foot of the bed. A bird twittered at the window, breaking the silence of the house. Above him, the fan ran in continuous, lazy circles. He was home.

Distress saturated every breath for a solid four minutes before Dave choked out, "Trey?" No answer came, and he croaked again, "Trey?"

Only the bird answered.

Dave let his head fall back onto the pillow. He was home and the throbbing in his legs evaporated with the dream. Breathe.

His chest rose and fell slowly, then again and again, working quickly until he pulled a pillow over his mouth. It did nothing to slow his breathing, but it muffled his screams.

Tears flowed unbidden and unwelcome, and he tried to jam them back into his eyes where they belonged. He forced his focus back to reality. He was home now. The war was over. They had won. The pain in his legs remained as a friendly reminder that he had not lost them.

As he had when stranded on the sidewalk, his body fought against panic, pain, and the overwhelming urge to empty his bladder. He'd drained it onto the ground then, but he had no desire to repeat the process in his bed.

He struggled onto his forearm, reaching for his chair. It sat on the other side of the nightstand, taunting him an inch from his fingertips. Trey had left it there, probably on purpose, so he didn't fall trying to get in by himself. He growled. If Trey wasn't going to let him get into his own wheelchair, he should be here to help him.

"Trey!"

Receiving no answer, Dave filled the silence with a string of curses. Last time he had fallen, his legs had hurt for days. He swallowed, concentrating as if he could use mental powers to draw the chair to his hand. He glared and gave up. He could wait—but not for long.

He closed his eyes, then opened them, afraid of falling asleep again. They had moved his bed downstairs when he first returned home. He had kept the window shutters drawn for a year until a storm ripped them off and allowed sunlight to barge into the room, but there was nothing of interest outside.

The back pasture lay bare, except for a tire that swung lazily from the tree. He'd spent hours on it as a kid. He'd even pushed Lucy on it, answering her cry of "faster, faster." He'd spun her in circles until the tree caught her hair, yanking a small section from her scalp. She'd cried, and he'd felt guilty for days.

He had more than compensated for her tears the day the wedding bells bragged about her marriage, taunting him until he'd screamed for Trey to close the windows. She would have married him when he returned. She'd said so in the letters. When she learned that he was a cripple, he had known things would change. He just hadn't expected her to turn to Sheldon for comfort and leave him to struggle on his own with an eleven-year-old kid as his only help.

Apparently, Trey had grown tired of helping. Dave shouldn't be angry. Trey was growing up and forming his own life. He couldn't be tied down all the time when he was already doing more than his share. Dave took a steadying breath to ward off the irritation. Trey could have left the stupid chair close enough for him to reach.

He growled and rolled onto his arms. If he could pull himself onto his nightstand, he could probably gain the few inches he needed to tug the chair to the bed. He could lower himself into it. He was crippled, not helpless. He nudged the lamp back until the shade hit the wall and carefully worked his body onto the surface of the table.

It shook and protested with creaks as he realized the flaw in the idea. The edge of the table jabbed into his ribs as he stretched, this time touching the arm of the chair. His heart lifted with hope as the chair turned an inch.

His lamp toppled onto the floor, scattering slivers of green glass in all directions. Dave cussed through clenched teeth as the shards slid under the wheels of the chair, hindering its journey toward him as it gleamed and taunted his impending fall. This was ridiculous. Stupid. The chair was right there at his fingertips, and he couldn't get himself into it.

"Stupid!" He shoved hard against the table to roll back onto the bed, groaning as the momentum ruined all chances of keeping his dignity. Once the flow started, he couldn't stop it. He cussed again as his pants and bedding grew wet.

All he wanted was to get up and get dressed like any normal person did every day of their lives. When was Trey coming back? Was he going to have to lie there in his own urine the entire day?

"Stupid idiot!" he hissed, unsure whether he was directing the name toward his brother or himself. By the time the front door slammed, his fists hurt from clenching. He kept his eyes plastered on the ceiling as he howled, "Trey, where have you been?"

A low whistle answered, and a mild Scottish accent floated into the room. "The boy went to church today. Surely you can't fault him for that."

Dave reached to yank the covers over his legs, hoping they'd cover the wet patch on the bed as William Barrie shuffled into the room.

"Laura sent the extra from the garden. I thought I'd drop it by. There's a basket on the table." The fan breeze lifted tufts of silver hair as his neighbor studied him. "No man deserves to be stranded in bed all day. Come on. Let's get you up."

William was growing too old to be lifting Dave, but he still worked his farm and took long walks across the fields. William was nearly as fit at sixty as he had been at forty.

Dave said nothing as the man rummaged through his dresser drawers to find fresh clothing. He grudgingly accepted help into clean clothes and then into the chair. William said nothing about the weakness of his legs or the mess, but Dave's jaw clenched harder when the man pulled off the sheets.

Remembering William's reply, Dave asked, "Why did Trey go to church?"

"I thought perhaps you could tell me that," William answered, dropping the sheets into the corner. "I heard he was there." The blue eyes twinkled. "I was glad to hear it, though I suspect that it has more to do with a girl than God."

*Girl?*

Trey going to church for a girl wouldn't surprise him, except that the boy had spent the last year or two moaning that he couldn't get one. Dave wheeled himself into the kitchen, hoping his visitor would follow. "What girl?"

"The reverend's granddaughter has just come into town. I think her name is Lily." William chuckled. "Laura spent all day yesterday on the party line."

Dave frowned. "Trey hasn't mentioned anything."

"The whole town's talking about her." William sat at the table, fingers tapping out a silent melody onto the wood. "He was probably just curious. He'll be back to your heathen ways before long."

Dave rolled himself closer to the window. "I'm not going back to church, Mr. Barrie, so don't try to talk me into it."

"I wouldn't." William's voice sounded surprised and sincere. "You can't force God on people." The man was quiet a moment. "Though it was good to hear your brother is trying again. Let him make up his own mind about his beliefs." He switched topics as he settled into a chair. "I'm going to need help shucking the corn this year. Will you be joining us again?"

Dave nodded. He'd helped the man every fall since he was a kid, so it didn't feel like a job given from pity.

William smiled. "Good. We're planning on putting that second field to work next season. I might have to hire a few more workers."

Dave glanced at the man to see if he was teasing. The best part about William's farm was that only the immigrant and his wife lived there. Laura was a soft-spoken, motherly woman. They were the closest thing to grandparents that the boys could remember.

"Oh," Dave said.

William wasn't much more of a talker than Dave and, after an awkward moment, he stood and picked up the basket. "Well, I'd best be on my way." His eyes sparkled as he warned, "You don't come down too hard on him, you hear? He's a good boy."

"Yeah," Dave muttered.

William shook his head like he knew nothing was going to sweeten his temper and shuffled out the door. Despite the warning, Dave's jaw clenched the moment he heard Trey's voice as William reached the bottom of the steps.

"Oh! Hi, Mr. Barrie!" Trey sounded guilty.

"Hi there, Trey. I brought you some vegetables from the garden. They're on the table."

"Thanks. Is Dave awake? He was asleep when I left."

"He's awake. Up and about."

"Oh."

Dave huffed before wheeling himself back to his bedroom.

Trey cowered in the kitchen, putting away the vegetables with the speed of an old woman. His footsteps slowed as he neared the room for a peek. "Hi, Dave."

Dave greeted him with a dry glare. "Next time you leave the house, leave the chair within reach."

Trey's mouth hung for a split second as he searched for some sort of defense before he replied, "Sorry. I didn't realize the service would last that long. I figured I'd be back before you woke up."

"Yeah, well, you weren't."

"Dave." Trey's voice took on the hurt, pleading tone that had worked when he was a kid but just sounded pathetic now.

Dave wheeled himself past the boy into the kitchen where he pretended to work on a radio. It was a hobby he had toyed with as a kid, creating a radio from scratch. He didn't really know how to tell what was wrong with various sets.

Trey scooted into a seat across from him with the stupidity of a kicked puppy. "Why are you mad?"

Dave flung down a screwdriver and the boy flinched. "I'm mad because I broke my lamp trying to get that stupid chair closer. If the house had caught fire, you'd be back living with Mr. and Mrs. Barrie, and I'd be dead."

Trey's eyes flickered to the top of the table before he murmured, "I'll fix your lamp."

"Don't bother. It's shattered," Dave said. "Just clean it up and throw it away."

Trey sighed as he rose to trudge into the bedroom.

Dave swallowed, realizing he'd completely forgotten to ask his brother about the girl.

# 4

Lila felt as stiff and suppressed as the starched collar that wrapped around Reverend Howard's red neck. It really wasn't fair. With her grandmother out of bed, there were now two adults frowning at her, and she wasn't even quite sure of what she had done.

Her grandfather pointed to a seat on the couch. "Sit down. We have some things to discuss."

"Sweetheart," Mrs. Howard began. "We love you, and we're so glad you're staying with us. We know you were raised much differently than how things are done here."

Lila kept her eyes to the window, bracing for the inevitable "but."

Reverend Howard supplied it. "But we have rules here, and you have managed to break nearly every one on your first morning. The most important rule is not to lie. I had no idea you were such a little liar."

Lila's eyes widened innocently. "You told me not to tell anything about Mom and Dad."

"Honey, we asked that you avoid certain subjects," her grandmother explained. "Not that you make up an elaborate story turning your father into a hero."

"Fine." Lila's eyebrows knotted and she openly glared. "Next time I'll tell them the truth."

"You'll tell them nothing at all!" Reverend Howard commanded before he took a breath. "Lila, we're trying to protect you."

Lila stood. "I never asked for your protection. I've been just fine on my own."

Reverend Howard wagged a finger at her. "I will not allow lying, especially to your grandmother or me. You are to go to school and listen to your teachers. You're to come straight home after lessons. Always ask permission before you go somewhere. Lila, are you listening?"

"My name's Delilah."

"I am not calling you 'Delilah.' You are Lila here."

Lila crossed her arms. "What's wrong with it?"

"It's not a good name."

"Why?"

"Because it's the name of a seductress, and I won't have it in my home."

Lila stared. What was the man talking about? "Well, it's still my name. And if you won't use my name, I won't listen to your rules." She fled up the same steps her mother had used in past decades.

Reverend Howard's voice grated as he called, "If you're going to your room, you can stay there all day."

"It's not my room," Lila shouted. "It's my mother's room, full of my mother's things!" She slammed the door, barricading herself before she leaned against it and rested her head back.

The room had stayed just the way it had been when Ruth left with Lila's father. Frilly white curtains and a soft pink quilt contrasted the personality of the woman she remembered. Her dresses had hung untouched in the closet until her daughter came along and was told she could wear them. As if Lila wanted to wear anything that belonged in the Depression.

She shoved the clothes to the side and hung up the few dresses that she brought from the orphanage, kicking her church clothing viciously into the corner. She'd never wear that again, no matter what her grandfather said. There wasn't much she could do about the shoes.

She pulled out a gray sailor dress with a wince. "Oh, Mama, how did you ever wear that?"

All of the clothing was so drab, she felt like she was still at the orphanage. If she knew how to sew, perhaps she could change the shape. She studied various pieces of clothing, wondering if a bit of dye would help. If she ruined the clothes trying to alter them, her grandparents would just have to get her something new. She couldn't go to school wearing *nothing*, though the idea made her grin.

She took a pair of scissors to a peach-colored dress. She had one day to pull together a decent outfit for school. Two if she wore her red dress tomorrow. She chewed the inside of her lip, wondering what the school would be like. It didn't seem appealing if the girls she met today were any indication. A small smile played across her face as she remembered their faces at the graveyard. The people in this town were so gullible.

Snatches of her grandparents' conversation floated through the door. Lila held still, holding her breath to listen. Her grandparents confused her as much as she seemed to worry them.

"She's been through so much, and she's only just arrived. Give her a little time, sweetheart. You can't come down too harshly yet." Mrs. Howard's voice grew shaky. "We'll lose her like we lost Ruth. She's just like her."

"Ruth wasn't like that until she met *him*. He raised Lila. What else can we expect?"

Lila frowned, yanking a hideous dress from the hanger. There was nothing wrong with her father. Nothing at all.

By the next morning, nearly every dress in the closet lay in a disastrous heap. Though she didn't feel a shred of remorse over ruining her mother's things in her quest to create a decent outfit, the fear of punishment sent her sneaking out before breakfast to avoid questioning.

She eased the screen shut, taking one step back and tripping over a box sitting on the porch. She cussed, dropping to her knees but only a squirrel inquired about the noise. The handwriting on the box's note was the worst that she'd ever seen, but the scrawls caught her attention.

*To Lila. For school.* It wasn't signed.

She snatched the gift and jogged down the driveway until bushes obstructed the view from the windows. Sitting in the grass, she glanced toward the empty street before turning her attention toward the package. It was wrapped in an old newspaper that declared the end of the war.

Inside lay a crisp pair of saddle shoes that she turned over and over in her hands. She bit her lip against a grin as she slid them over the hole in her sock. They were one size too big, and it wasn't likely that her feet would grow anymore.

*"Aschenputte fusse,"* her father had always teased. *"Cinderella feet."* She grinned as she stuffed the toes of the shoes with the newspaper shreds. Looking more down than up on her way to the school, she escaped puddles and gum, finding an odd pleasure in the stiffness of the leather. Never had she owned a pair of shoes that came straight from a box.

Her father had presented secondhand pairs that he had found and cleaned up, along with a story about how they had been worn by someone famous who had gifted them to her. She had played along with his game, knowing full well that they were only tokens of a man who did the best he could. Like the shoes with the heels he had mended or tied with laces from his own boots, life had not been kind to Ralph.

"Lila!" A voice snapped her out of her memories. Her father's face faded and was replaced by the ice cream boy. What was his name? Trey. It was Trey.

"Hi." Her eyes slit, roving down the deserted yards. "Is this your regular route?"

"No." Trey swung into an easy gait beside her. "I just thought you might need help finding the school."

"I don't." He seemed almost disappointed, and it amused her. She continued, "But once I get there, it would be nice to have someone point out my classes."

"I can do that." He said it the same way that he had offered the root beer.

With anyone else, it would be annoying to be perceived as naive enough to fall for the "extra float" story, but with him, it was just plain adorable. She subtly eyed his shoes, finding them almost as worn as the donations stowed in her book bag. He couldn't replace his own shoes. He wouldn't have bought any for her.

She pushed the mystery from her mind, hinting, "I didn't see you at church last night."

"Oh. Yeah. I don't go at night." He scratched the back of his neck, squinting into the sun. "I stayed with Dave."

"Who is Dave?"

"He's my brother."

"How old is he?"

"Um, twenty-four." Trey kicked a rock out of the road. "He was crippled during the war."

Lila winced and changed the subject. "So, besides dancing, what is there to do for fun around here?"

Trey huffed a laugh. "Not much. The fair will be here next month. That's pretty fun, but it's only a week."

"Is there a movie theater?"

"Nope." Trey shook his head. "There used to be. Most of the businesses closed during the war and never started up again. Actually, only eleven of twenty-seven guys who shipped out came back. The man who owned the movie theater lost all four sons and ended up killing himself."

"Geez." Lila winced. "I guess I wouldn't want to go to that theater anyway. It's probably haunted."

"Have you ever been? To a theater, I mean?" Trey asked.

"No." Lila shook her head.

Trey glanced sideways. "There's one over in Breeze City. Maybe we could go there sometime. It's about forty-five minutes away." He squinted against the sun as he talked. "Though I guess your grandpa wouldn't let you do that either. Why can't you dance?"

"I don't know," Lila answered. "My grandfather just said I couldn't go to the Soda Shoppe. He didn't say why, but in a town this small, I can't exactly sneak around."

Trey turned to walk backwards in front of her. "What about dancing itself? Would you like it?"

"Yes." Lila hesitated. "What kind though?"

"Swing. I could teach you." Trey's eyes sparkled as every feature on his face perked. "I've been thinking. We have this—"

The school bell interrupted whatever he'd been thinking.

Trey grabbed Lila's hand, yanking her into a sprint. "Come on! Principal Gordon's really strict about being late."

They reached the steps as the principal shut the door, waiting until they knocked before he graced them with a hearing. He was a small man with glasses so tiny they looked useless. He pointed to his watch. "It's nine o'clock."

"I'm sorry," Trey said, panting through thick breaths that made him sound more tired than sorry.

Lila stepped up. "It's my fault. I was lost. Trey saw me on the corner headed the wrong way and chased me down."

The door opened a little wider. "I'll make an exception today. I trust you'll be able to find it on time tomorrow?"

"Yes, sir. Thank you." She sent the man a charming smile as they passed.

Trey looked as guilty as if he had lied to the principal. He sputtered before saying, "Come on. I'll show you to class."

Once inside the classroom, Lila was forced to the front desk to stare down a small army of eyes as she was introduced. Trey slipped into the third row from the front, blending in with the other good boys of average intelligence.

Lila received instructions to sit by a girl who wore so much perfume she could knock a person out with one whiff. She was four seats down from Trey, but still close enough to observe his shoes tapping lightly beneath the desk. Trey wasn't kidding when he said he was a dancer.

As the hours passed, Lila breezed through history by interest, English by daydreaming, and algebra by subtly copying steps and answers from various papers within sight. Trey didn't seem to be having much trouble with the assignments, and she wished she was sitting close enough to see his work.

Perhaps she could ask him for help later. She wasn't stupid. She just hadn't stayed in school for more than a few months at a time when she was young. In the orphanage, she was too worried about survival to expend energy learning numbers and facts. She scribbled drawings of birds and flowers during the last class.

All sorts of stories circulated about her past and parentage, ranging from vicious to just plain stupid. The looks and giggles didn't faze Trey, who stayed near her side every spare moment of the day. He pointed out every class whether she needed it or not, warned about or praised various passing students, offered to carry her books, and opened every door she stepped through.

After school, she exiled her homework to the recesses of her book bag and rushed away from the flocks of students, secretly relieved that the day was done. She waited in the schoolyard until Trey emerged from the masses. He didn't seem in a hurry, so she asked, "Do you work today?"

"No." Trey glanced sideways at her. "Did you want to do homework together?"

She should say "yes" and ask him about those math problems that had letters sprinkled in with the numbers, but there was nothing exciting about the prospect, so she dropped her pack to sit on the ground. "No. I just got out of school."

Trey kicked the curb as she pulled her shoe off. "Why are you changing your shoes?"

"I don't want to ruin these."

"Oh." His hands went into his pockets. "Are those new?"

"Yeah. Somebody left them on my porch."

"Who?"

"I don't know." She glanced toward him, but he seemed just as curious as she was. "I don't really care. They're mine now."

He laughed.

She placed them in the book bag and donned the gray ones. "I'm hiding them though. My grandfather might say they're evil or something and take them away." She surveyed the houses around them. "Do you have any rivers around here? Creeks? Bodies of water larger than a puddle?"

"There's a river out by my place. Do you want to see it?"

"Yes." She had instructions to go home, but she didn't want her grandfather getting too comfortable giving her orders. She was a big girl. She could find her way home before dinner.

Trey led Lila out of town, cutting across the back fields, elated at the prospect of spending an afternoon with her. "We'll take the shortcut. It passes behind my house."

Lila slung the book bag over her free shoulder. "Since it's near your house, can we leave our things there? It would be better than hauling it."

Trey nodded. "Yeah. I've got to check on Dave anyway."

Lila's mouth perked. "Do I get to meet him?"

"No. Probably not."

"Why not?"

"He doesn't like people seeing him."

She actually smiled. "What? Is he some creature that only comes out at night?"

"No. He just doesn't like people seeing him crippled." Trey turned onto the dirt road that led home. It took a lot longer to walk than it did to ride his bike. "So how did your grandparents find you? Where did you go after your parents died?"

Lila's face swung away from him, though she shrugged lightly. "I've been in an orphanage for a few years now."

"Really?" Trey had wondered many times what his life would have been like if Dave had died too. It was bad enough to lose his family. He couldn't imagine losing his home. "How come your grandparents didn't get you?"

"They didn't know I existed. You didn't hear the story?" Lila matched his stride, bumping him toward the road. "How my evil father came and seduced my mother from family, friends, and common sense?" Her eyes widened. "She was kidnapped, you know. Under a full moon."

Trey smirked. "I heard something like that, but I want to know the truth. Your grandparents didn't know about you at all?"

"No."

Trey waited for her to give more details, but Lila seemed more interested in locating the squirrel that screamed at them from a tree. He searched for another subject. "What was the orphanage like?"

She shrugged. "It ran off charity. It had lice and mice and cracks in the walls. We had a bomb drill every week. Sometimes parts of the ceiling plaster fell, so it seemed like there really was an attack."

"And you just got out?"

"Last week." She glanced toward her shoes. "Hence the grubby clothes."

"Do you miss your friends there?"

She shook her head. "Opal was my best friend since I got there, and she died from polio. Danny was my best guy friend, but he turned eighteen and was released. He was going to come for me when I was released, but after six months I stopped hearing from him." She huffed a laugh. "They probably confiscated our letters. I got in trouble all the time there without even trying."

Trey winced. "Being here should be a relief then. Even your grandfather can't be that strict."

Her eyes slanted. "Not really. I hate hearing them talk about my dad the way they do. He wasn't the bad guy everyone thinks. He took care of us." She darted off the path to snag an apple from the tree on the edge of the Barries' farm.

Trey frowned. William wouldn't mind, but she still didn't have permission to go apple-picking.

She ate it without remorse before she asked, "Want to know a secret?"

Trey perked. "What's that?"

"My name's not Lila."

"It's not?"

"Nope."

"What is it?"

"It's Delilah."

"Oh, so Lila's your nickname?"

"No." She shifted her book bag to her other shoulder. "Lila is what my grandfather said I had to go by because he doesn't like Delilah."

"Why not?"

"He said she was an evil seductress, I guess in the Bible or something." She picked up a stick to beat at the passing weeds. "Do you know that story?"

"Uh-uh." Trey shook his head. It sounded interesting though. "I didn't know they had stories like that in the Bible."

"I didn't either," Lila grinned. "I didn't think the Bible was that exciting."

Trey turned down the driveway to his home, wondering if the story was worth searching through such a large book. "Come on. Just dump your bag on the porch. You can get it when we come back." He should leave before she got interested, but he needed to check on Dave. "I'll be back. I'm just going to—"

Lila sprinted up the steps. "Let me go, too. I want to meet him."

"No!" Trey scooted between her and the door. "No, you can't."

She cocked her head and a corner of her mouth. "Why? You said he wasn't scary."

"No, it's just . . . Stop!"

Trey slammed a hand against the screen as Lila reached for the handle. Lila tightened her grip, angling her body to block him. Her eyes turned stormy.

"Trey, what is your problem?"

Geez, the girl could be scary. Trey released the handle and backed off, watching helplessly as Lila disappeared into the house. By the time he followed, Dave and Lila were eyeing each other across the kitchen table like two tomcats meeting in a back alley.

Dave's eyes snapped to him. "What's she doing here?"

"We were just dropping our things off," Trey sputtered.

"And I decided I wanted to meet you." Lila stuck her hand into the air between them like she was a man. "I'm Delilah. Lila, if you're in town."

Dave's eyes darkened. "I don't go to town."

Her mouth softened into the slightest smile. "You're a smart man. I wouldn't either if I could help it."

The reply startled Dave enough to derail his comeback.

Lila settled into a chair, smoothing out her skirt. "Those people in town. They're crazy as hootie owls. Especially that boy down at the ice cream shop."

A smile crept around Dave's mouth. "You think so?"

"Um-hum." Lila's hair bobbed with her chin. "You have to watch that one."

"We were going to the river," Trey said, stepping closer to the table. Seeing Dave's eyes glint, he added, "If that's okay with you. I can stay if you need help."

"I don't need help," Dave growled.

Trey backed toward the door. "Sorry." He glanced at the girl. "Ready?"

"You could come," Lila said to Dave.

Dave shook his head. "No."

"No, really. We could push you." She stood and circled his chair, but Dave inched it further beneath the table to shield his legs.

"No."

"We'll go somewhere where we can push your chair."

"No."

She frowned, completely ignoring the warning tone that made Trey back away. "Oh, come on! When was the last time you got out of this house?"

Dave's jerked away from the table. "Get out."

Lila stepped back with a sigh. "Come on, Trey."

As she left, Dave caught Trey's hand, forcing eye contact before he said, "Don't bring her back here."

Trey nodded, then followed the girl. He wasn't sure he could keep her from coming back if she wanted to return, but he could try to keep her interested in something outside of the house.

He took quick strides to catch up. "Hey. Instead of swimming, do you want to dance?"

Lila turned, appraising him solemnly. "We'd be in trouble if we got caught."

"Better not get caught then." He worked a crooked smile that he hoped covered his nerves. "Come on. I'm not asking you on a date. Just a dance." He jutted his chin. "We could dance in the barn. No one has to know."

Lila cocked one eyebrow, playfully folding her arms. "And if we did get caught? What would you do about it?"

"I'd . . ." He didn't know. He didn't normally break rules. He'd never even been to the principal's office. "I'd explain it was all my fault, and I talked you into it."

She huffed a laugh. "Okay."

Trey scampered back up the steps for the smallest working radio he could find, hauling it to the barn. Lila peeked into the stalls and scaled the ladder as Trey worked the knobs to find a station that came in semi-clear.

"Why don't you have animals?" she asked.

"They're too much work. We sold them after my dad died."

"Too bad. I was hoping you'd have horses."

"I never liked our horses," Trey replied. "They bit. Dave was pretty good with them though."

Lila stood at the edge of the loft, surveying the barn. "So how long has it been since Dave was out of the house?"

"A long time. A few years. Why'd you push him like that?"

"All invalids should be shaken up now and then."

He stared. "I can't believe you just called him that."

"An invalid?" She climbed down, jumping the last three rings. "Would you prefer convalescent?"

"How about 'Dave'? He's not an object. He's a person who got hurt."

"I know." Her eyes widened slightly. "They're called invalids." She moved past him to fine-tune the music. "That's a good song. So how do we do this?"

Dancing. They were dancing, not discussing his brother. Trey reached for her hands. "Okay. Your feet mirror mine. So, step right, step left." He showed her with his feet. "Step back, then back in place."

She walked slowly through the steps with him. "Like this?"

"Yes. No." He tapped her right foot with his shoe. "That one goes back."

"Oh." She performed the steps correctly.

He walked her through the basic swing steps, pleased at how well she caught on. She would be the perfect partner. She was the right height, the right size, and her hands were really warm and soft.

Song after song went by until he was spinning her, aching to pick her up, but he couldn't rush her too much, either in the dance or the relationship. After a particularly fast song by

Benny Goodman, they swung to a halt.

Trey laughed. "Geez, I think you danced me out. I haven't done this for a while."

"I thought you were the big dancer around town." Lila smirked as she sat on an overturned milk bucket.

"Well, I was," Trey mumbled. "It's just been a while."

"Why?"

He blushed, then spread his arms. "I've been waiting for you, babe."

She laughed, but only replied, "This is fun, Trey."

"Yeah." He sank onto the floor, resting his arms on his knees.

Lila asked, "Are you sure you're not just dancing with me because I'm short like you?"

"I'm very sure." Trey glanced over. "I like you."

She grinned. "Many have."

Trey's smile faded. "At the orphanage?"

"No. Only one at the orphanage. Well, two, but I only liked one back well enough to marry."

Something panged in Trey's stomach. "Who were they?"

"Josh and Jacob," she answered lightly. "Jacob ran away."

Trey wondered which she had liked back enough to marry. "And where's Josh?"

She shook her head. "I don't know. Last time I saw him, he was wearing black leather and zooming by on a motorcycle." She took a breath. "Not exactly someone my grandfather would approve."

"I'm not sure he'd approve of anyone."

"Probably not. Especially not guys who lure me into doing forbidden things."

Trey flushed. "Dancing's not really bad. You're having fun, aren't you?"

Lila laughed. "More than I ever have."

They danced until the sun began to slip like sand through an hourglass, reminding them that their homes had people waiting on them. Supper smelled awful by the time Trey stepped into the kitchen.

Dave had cooked blindly on the stove, stirring a pot at his eye level. He could have scalded himself but scolding wouldn't do any good now. Trey moved toward the table and began filling his plate.

Dave asked, "How was the river?"

"We didn't go."

"So where were you all day?"

"Um, just around." He glanced sidelong at his brother. "Are you all right?"

Dave rubbed the back of his head. "I've got to hand it to you. You sure picked a strange one."

"She's not strange. She's . . ."

"Short?"

Trey grinned slightly. "That's not why I picked her."

"Good." Dave's eyes met his. "Because her grandmother came over today asking if she was here."

Trey's heart slowed. They hadn't heard anyone from their hideout in the barn. He carried a bowl of beans to the table. "What did you say?"

"I told her that she wasn't here." Dave rolled a screw between his fingers. "She's not allowed to dance."

"I know." Trey's face pricked.

"I'm only warning you."

"We're just friends." Trey stuck a forkful of beans into his mouth, then choked and spit them out. "Gah, Dave, those are awful!"

"I know." Dave's eyebrows rose.

Trey moved to scrape his plate into the trash. "I'll get something from the diner."

"If you go to the diner, you won't be home for three hours."

"Yeah, I will."

Dave sighed. "No, you won't."

Trey spun. "I . . . fine. I'll stay and starve since you're so *lonely*."

Dave looked like he might protest before he closed his mouth again, turning back to the radio.

Trey flopped into a chair, feet tapping on the floor. He'd have another boring night at home.

A clear voice carried from the speaker, and Dave smiled as he slapped the table. "There! It's fixed."

"It's about time," Trey muttered.

Dave continued undeterred, "You can tell Mrs. Miller you'll bring it by."

"Okay," Trey answered.

Dave shoved back, softening a little. "You okay?"

"Yeah, I'm fine." Trey pulled off his shoes, wincing at the toe that protruded from a sock. "Just bored and hungry."

"Tell me about it," Dave muttered.

Trey nearly asked him why he didn't come today, but he couldn't work up the nerve. If he was the eldest, he'd order Dave outside. They could work the legs and keep them from getting worse. Maybe Dave could even walk again. Trey glanced at the man. Then again, maybe not.

He snagged a rubber band, looping it around his fingers with an evil grin and snapped it toward Dave. Dave caught it, positioning it on his finger as Trey jumped up, retreating behind the safety of his bedroom door.

"No fair!" Dave called.

Trey flopped onto his bed. He had homework. He'd spent

the whole day with Lila until she'd run home. The girl could run like a deer. It was incredible.

Just as his thoughts began to fill with her, his door opened. A pillow sailed across the room, landing squarely on his face.

"Ow!" Trey howled a laugh, grabbing his own pillow and hurled it back at Dave.

It wasn't exactly a fair fight, but it was a fun one, especially when Dave retreated into the bathroom where he abandoned the pillow and went for a bottle of shaving cream.

"Hey! No fair!" Trey grabbed the toothpaste, but it didn't work as well. When the bathroom was more of a mess than it had ever been, they removed the soaked pillowcases. Mother wasn't here to scold them. He'd have a heck of a mess to clean, but at least Dave had laughed himself into a good mood.

Trey climbed onto his bed again, drawing his legs up against his chest. "What would you say to me going to church again next Sunday?"

Dave's eyebrow went up. "It doesn't matter what I think, does it? Just look out for lightning bolts if you're only going to see that girl. And make sure I'm up before you leave."

"Okay." Trey leaned against his slightly stained and very damp pillow.

Dave smirked. "What? You want a bedtime story?"

"Oh, yes. The one about the magic beans." Trey made his voice childlike. "And the big scary wolf."

"That's two."

"Well, isn't there one about a bean and a big scary wolf?"

Dave shook his head, backing toward the door. "You're a weird kid."

"Hey, Dave." Trey rolled onto his stomach, resting his cheek on his hand. "Do you know why your car won't start?"

Dave hesitated. "Not exactly."

Trey studied his fingers. "I was thinking if we got it working, we could go places in it."

"Go places in a car." Dave's fingers gripped his chair, belying the smile he pulled onto his face. "Imagine that."

Trey tossed the pillow. "Come on. I'm being serious. Can we get it working?"

Dave caught the pillow, dropping it into his lap to smooth out. "I don't know." The silence stretched as he petted the pillow, straightening the corners like it was a shirt collar he was getting ready to iron. His jaw worked before he swallowed. "If you can work on it, I can probably tell you what to do."

That was a "yes." He'd have his own car. Trey tried not to act too excited. "Yeah. Let's do that."

Dave nodded and wheeled himself backward through the door. The strained note hadn't quite left his voice before he asked, "This wouldn't have anything to do with the new girl, would it?"

"Huh?" Trey's face pricked. "No. No, I've been thinking about it for a while. I mean, it's just rusting out there."

Dave's eyes glistened but he said, "We'll see about it."

Trey ignored the guilt, imagining himself behind the wheel. He plotted dates with Lila and victorious races with Joe, crowding his mind with images to push away the lingering thought. *What would it be like to never drive again?*

# 5

The next day, a pair of new black and white shoes met a pair of scuffed canvas Converses on the melting asphalt. Lila fell into step beside Trey, swinging a book as she asked, "So how much trouble did you get into for staying out until supper?"

"None." Trey shook his head. "But Dave tried to make dinner himself, and that's never a good idea. He can't see what he's doing. It was bad. I was hungry all night."

She curled her bottom lip. "Poor Trey."

"What about you?" Trey glanced toward her. "Did you get into trouble?"

"Not much." She shrugged. "I'm supposed to come straight home after school today. My grandmother will probably force me to embroider in the living room so she can keep an eye on me."

"Really?" Trey felt his own face prick for her, but Lila kept walking like it didn't bother her a bit. "I didn't mean to get you into trouble. We should have stopped by your house first and—"

"They wouldn't have let me go," she interrupted. "I'm not worrying about it. I'm sixteen. I have two more years until I can live on my own. I'm not staying here."

Trey hadn't thought about being on his own after graduation. His life would change very little after high school.

He'd work full-time and then come home to Dave. "Where are you going to go?"

"To find my dad."

Trey blinked. "You said your dad was dead."

"I lied." She cut her eyes sideways. "Don't tell."

Trey stopped, staring after her. "Why would you lie about that?"

"Because my grandparents hate him. It's better if they can pretend he's dead."

"So where is he really?"

"I don't know." Her eyes flickered to her shoes. "He disappeared during the war."

"Oh." Trey frowned, wondering if she'd lied about her mother, too. "Like a POW?"

"Yeah. I guess."

"I'm sorry." He couldn't help asking. "But what makes you think he's alive?"

"Just a hunch, but even if he's not, I want to know why he never came back. You know?"

"Yeah. That's what happened to the Barries with Luke."

"What? Who are they?"

"Our neighbors. Luke and Dave weren't buddies or anything, but they were in school together. They shipped out at the same time, but Luke disappeared during the war, and nobody knows what happened to him. Mrs. Barrie burned a candle in her window for two years so he could find the house if he ever came home at night."

"Can you imagine what it would have been like if he had returned?" Lila's mouth perked, almost dreamily. "What it would be like to walk up the drive and realize somebody had left a candle burning just for you?"

He hadn't, but he did now, imagining walking home in a

dusty army uniform after two years of harrowing escapes. The old farmhouse looked worse than ever without a man to care for it, but the window was clean, and on the other side, Lila stood lighting a candle. She looked up, saw him, and they both ran, meeting on the front porch. She stood on her tiptoes because he'd grown so much and lifted her lips to—

"Hey, soda boy!"

Trey resisted a moan. He'd walked too slowly past Joe's street. The teen strode up, flipping a lighter. Joe was one step ahead of Michael, both physically and mentally. He confiscated Trey's book bag in one smooth motion.

"On your way to school, I see. Whatcha got in here?"

Trey lurched for the bag, clawing the air as Joe swung it away. He should tackle the boy. Throw him to the ground, claim his bag, and—

"Whoo. Somebody's been a good little boy and done his homework. I'll take that." Joe pulled out the papers and handed them to Michael.

"Stop," Trey protested. "Come on. Give it back. You can't use it anyway."

Michael stepped closer until his chest was at Trey's face. "Yeah? Good point." He shredded Trey's papers. "What'cha going to do about it?"

"Hey!" Lila snapped. She hurled her book, bashing Joe in the face. "Give it back, you jerk!"

Joe hooted. "Oh, oh! So you got your little dame doing your fighting, huh?"

It was stupid to fight them. Trey would never win and the homework was already ruined, but when Joe grabbed Lila, what choice did he have?

Trey ducked his head and plowed into the guy's stomach. He got in two good punches before he panicked, feeling Joe's arms close around his middle. His feet went over his head, and he watched the sidewalk rise to crash into his face and chest. He grabbed Joe's legs before the guy could kick him.

Michael jumped onto his back as if he was going to ride a horse. Trey used all 120 pounds of himself to push up, but he was trapped. His legs flailed. The boys hooted. Joe caught his arms, and he was stuck.

He stayed stuck until a pair of black and white shoes landed next to his eyes.

Michael lurched forward, caught off-guard. "What the—" Michael launched to his feet, and Trey could breathe again.

Lila wrapped her arms around Michael's neck, clamping her legs around his waist. Michael clawed at her arms, but Lila stayed on his back like a monkey until he caught her hair and yanked her head forward. She fought back like a wildcat by biting his shoulder.

"Let her go!" Trey screamed.

Joe twisted Trey's arm, threatening to free his shoulder from the socket. All over a stupid piece of homework. When Joe rolled him onto his back, Trey glimpsed the sky before a fist blotted it out. The colors ate each other, swallowing, moving like some weird creature. His hands were pinned. He couldn't shield his face, though he certainly felt it being mashed before the fist moved down his chest to his stomach.

Enraged, he squirmed until he freed a hand, managing to catch the wrist. He heard Lila screaming rather obscene names. She must be faring better than he was, but she was in pain. Man, oh man. He was going to go blind and lose all of his teeth. Everyone would laugh, she'd never speak to him again, and *why* wouldn't the guy get off him? He felt kicks to his ribs, but he couldn't see because his eyes were either swelled shut or full of blood.

Even after the laughter and footsteps faded, he couldn't move. He choked, rolled, and spat dirt and blood onto the grass. The colors swirled into blackness as he fought to stay alert.

Lila touched his shoulder. "Trey?"

He looked toward the voice before remembering he didn't want her seeing him.

Lila swore something that almost sounded like another language through the ringing in his ears. "Trey?"

Dirt fell from his ear as he reached up to touch the side of his face, finding his skin puffy and sticky. Why was this happening around the one person he wanted to impress the most? He heard a ripping sound before a dry cloth dabbed at his eye.

"Gosh, those eyes," Lila said. "We've got to get you home before they swell all the way shut."

Weren't they *already* shut? Trey stumbled to his feet, but he couldn't see and his legs wobbled until he caught her arms. "Are you okay?" he asked, peering through his blurred vision. "Did they—"

"I'm fine!" Lila pushed against his shoulders. "Stay down. I'm going to call somebody."

Dave couldn't come and get him. It would be a long walk home in this state. Trey spat more blood. "Can you call Mr. Barrie?"

"Yeah." She pushed his shoulders until he sat. "Hold on. I'll find a phone. Don't go anywhere."

As if he could. What if they came back? His ears burned. This would be all over town in an hour. His face had settled into a stinging throb by the time Lila returned. They hid in the bushes until William's truck rumbled to the curb.

The Scottish charm was missing from his voice as the man's cool fingers gripped Trey's elbow. "That was quite the brawl, wasn't it, boy? Come on. Let's get you into the truck."

Trey stumbled blindly, catching only snatches of conversation. His head throbbed, his face ached, and his stomach churned until he scooted away from Lila. Every bump of the truck made him want to whimper, but he held his breath instead.

Lila patted his leg and whispered, "On the upside, we got out of morning classes."

Later, that might help. Now, all he could think about was what an idiot he must look like. Blind was something he never wanted to be, he discovered, as Lila led him up the steps into the Barries' house.

"Oh, Trey!" Laura's accent wasn't Scottish, but it had a slight lilt that she must have picked up from her husband. Trey had never realized how young her voice still sounded when not accompanied by the laugh lines around her eyes or the gray hair that she still wore in a coiled braid, instead of a short perm like every other woman in town. She ushered him into a chair. "Sit down. Poor boy. We'll get you all cleaned up."

He wasn't sure he wanted the woman's mothering while his girlfriend was around, but he couldn't hear Lila. Maybe she had gone back out with William. Whatever Laura spread onto his face both soothed and stung. She dabbed gently at his eyes, then handed him something cold and hard. "Here. Hold this against your nose. Don't talk. Your lip will start bleeding again."

Trey complied until Laura began to unbutton his shirt.

"It's all right. Don't fret." Laura's voice floated into his ears, and he could nearly picture the sympathetic look on her face. "We're going to get your shirt off. It's soiled."

"Soiled" was an understatement. "Soaked" might be a better description. Laura wouldn't have anything soiled in her house for long without cleaning it, but what was he supposed to wear to cover his lack of defined muscles?

"Oh, dear," she said. He winced as she slid his shirt off his arms, and the cold farmhouse air hit his skin. "Poor boy. You're black and blue all over. Who did this? Never mind now. Don't speak. We'll hear about it soon enough. Whoever it is, you can be sure I'm having a chat with his mother."

A chat. That would help.

Trey stifled the bitter retort, seething silently as she worked. He should have slugged Joe years ago while they were closer to the same size. He coaxed one eye open a slit, testing his sight as Laura washed out the rag at the sink.

"I think you'd better stay here for a while. You can lie on Luke's bed or the couch if you'd rather."

He shifted in the wooden chair. "Where's Lila?"

"She's with William, I think. They should be in at any moment. I'm going to call your school and let them know you won't be there."

Trey sat back, holding ice to his eye as he listened to Laura talk.

The screen opened, and Lila's voice accompanied William's footsteps. "So they tore up his homework, and I slammed my book against Joe's face. He grabbed me, and then we all started fighting. Trey tried, but he couldn't hold two people off, you know. He was outnumbered because I don't count for a guy, and once they got him down they . . . did that." Her voice trailed off, and he had the distinct feeling that they were looking at him.

William moved closer until all Trey could see were the buttons on his shirt. "Well, they're gone now, but we'll talk to the sheriff. They can't go around beating people up. Trey, let's get you to the couch."

"Lila." Trey squirmed under her gaze in his scantily clad state. "Are you okay?"

"Who, me? Yeah. I have a few bruises and lost a few hairs, but I discovered long ago that my teeth and nails are my best allies." She laughed as if she'd enjoyed the whole thing. At least she hadn't told William that he had been flung to the ground and sat on while they had their merry little way with him.

William shuffled off after he got Trey onto the couch, leaving Lila. She knelt beside Trey, whispering, "Gosh, Trey. I'm sorry. I didn't mean to get you pounded like that."

"Wasn't your fault," he answered. Even though it sort of was. He managed not to flinch as she touched his face.

"When do you think you'll be able to see again?" she asked.

"I don't know. I can't see how bad it is. It'll probably go away in a day or two." He hoped. He couldn't miss too much school—or work for that matter.

"I don't know. Mr. Barrie's talking about taking you to the hospital to get those cuts fixed."

"No, he can't!" Trey whispered. "We can't afford that."

"I don't think he's expecting you to pay for it."

"He can't afford it either," Trey answered. "Just downplay it. It'll be fine." He couldn't tell what she was doing, so he tried to open his eyes wider.

She was looking at his chest. Admiring it? No, it wasn't admiration on her face. It was concern.

"Do you know those boys?" she asked.

"Yeah. They go to our school," Trey answered. "They've always been jerks."

"Do they always pick on you?"

"No," he lied.

"Good. We'd better get someone to come down on them hard."

"We don't need the adults."

Her eyebrows rose. "Yeah. We do. I can't take them on."

Trey couldn't either. She was kind not to say it.

William returned with a blanket. "There. Cover yourself. There are ladies present."

Lila giggled and whispered, "He's just jealous."

Now that the danger was gone, Lila manned the ice and rags so dotingly that it was hard to believe she was the same girl who had fought like a wild creature. Laura brought aspirin and gave him some sort of tea that made him sleepy. Voices faded in and out as he dozed on the couch.

"How long have you and Mr. Barrie lived here?" Lila asked.

Laura chuckled. "William grew up here after coming to America. I came in the twenties after we married."

"Where were you before?"

"I lived over in Breeze City. My father was a banker. William came in to pay off his father's loan one day while I was there, and I thought he was simply smashing. Of course, my father wasn't very happy about me marrying a farmer, but William's always been good to me and Luke."

"That's the boy in the picture? Luke?"

"Yes. That's my baby. He was such a sweet little boy."

"He looks like a nice guy."

Sleep pulled at Trey, but he resisted it when he heard Laura ask, "Where are you from, Lila?"

He expected a lie, but after a moment Lila replied, "I'm not supposed to talk about it."

"I see." Laura didn't inquire further. "Well, we're glad to have you, no matter where you came from. I had a rather lonely childhood, too."

Lila's voice perked with curiosity. "What do you mean?"

"Oh." Laura set a plate of cookies in front of her. "I was an only child. My father was a good man but very concerned about appearances. He enforced a lot of rules."

"Did you obey them?" Lila asked.

"Oh, yes. I rarely purposely disobeyed anything, at least until I became a woman and started making my own choices."

Lila huffed a laugh. "I purposely disobey all the time." Her voice softened. "Not my father, though. He didn't give stupid rules."

She blew out a breath as the screen opened and William stepped through. Trey resented the intrusion into his eavesdropping, but it was getting too hard to stay awake anyway.

"Time to be ending the chat," Mr. Barrie said. "The little miss must go to school."

For once, the little miss obeyed.

# 6

It had been years since Trey put up this sort of fight over going to bed. The boy was bruised, battered, and temporarily blinded, but he absolutely would not stay in one place. He paced the rooms until he ran into the furniture. Dave gritted his teeth. His brother was hurt, and he felt badly that it had happened.

He wouldn't admit his fears that it would happen again. Trey didn't need that right now. Trey needed ice, aspirin, a mother to dote over him, and a father to tell him to stay put or else. Dave had spent two days repeating orders to sit or lie on the bed, and his short fuse was sputtering.

"I don't want to," Trey spat. "I want to dance. I want to get out of the house. You can't expect me to sit around all day!"

"Trey, Mr. Barrie said you needed to keep your eyes shut. Even if you can partially see out of one, you shouldn't. Give it time to heal."

Trey glared at him through his slit eye.

Dave glared back. "Just go lie on your bed. You can listen to the radio."

"I'm not going to spend my life in bed!"

"It's not your life. It's a few days."

"Nobody spends days in bed, Dave."

"I spent months in bed, Trey!" Dave snapped. "You can manage an evening. Go."

Trey grumbled for another half-hour, then flopped onto the couch and tap-danced his feet against the wall.

Dave tried to ignore the noise. He didn't normally work on accounts while Trey was around, but his brother couldn't see anyway. Still, the tapping feet made it harder to concentrate on the rows of numbers; how much they had spent, where they could cut, and the never-ending debt. Trey would be graduating before they knew it. He needed money for college.

Dave blew out a frustrated breath. If he could walk, he could work. He had many skills, but none that could be done from a wheelchair.

A timid knock made him jump as a soft voice called out. "Hello?"

*Martha.*

Dave swallowed, closing his book, and pushing his chair further under the shadows of the table as the girl let herself inside the house.

Her smile was timid and almost apologetic. "Hi. I heard about Trey. Is he all right?"

Dave glanced over, but Trey was either asleep or a heck of a good faker. "He will be."

Martha eyed the kitchen. "I hope so. Can I... well, I figured..." She moved toward the stove, sucking in a breath. "I'm making you supper. Trey won't feel like doing it, I'm sure, and I just happened to have an evening free."

"That's kind, but..." Dave sputtered.

But what? He couldn't convince her that he could make it when his face was barely above the stove. Laura had brought a casserole when they brought Trey home, but they'd nearly finished it.

"That's kind of you," he finished.

"Oh, it's no problem at all." Martha rummaged through mismatched dishes in the cupboards. "I love to cook. Really. Besides, I had nothing else going on tonight." She seemed to run out of things to say, so she moved to the empty refrigerator. "I see you don't cook here much. I guess Trey probably brings food from the diner, right?" She peeked into the pantry. "Oh, good!" Her voice muffled as she disappeared inside. "I can work with this. We'll have a meal in no time."

She carried some of William's potatoes to the counter and scrounged for a pan. "So, how have you been, Dave?"

Better than he was now.

"I'm okay," Dave said. "I can help if you need."

Martha shook her head on her way to the sink where an overload of dishes obstructed her mission of getting water. "Oh, no. No, I have it. Actually . . ." She turned as sudden inspiration struck. "You can cut the carrots."

He could cut vegetables. Very helpful. At least it gave him something to hold his focus. Dave wheeled himself to fetch a knife, working silently in hope that she would too. She didn't.

"Well," she said. "I could catch you up on everyone in town. Or maybe Trey already has." She pulled her hair behind her ear before she carved the skin from a potato. "I've been teaching piano lessons for a few years now. Sammy Watson's boy is catching on real fast. They're teasing him about being a musical genius. Personally, I don't think he is, though he could put me out of business when he gets older. Oh, and Tyler. You remember him from school, right? Well, he's working at the auto parts store now, and he's talking about leaving us and going to Los Angeles. Wouldn't that be something? Someone from this town going to a big city like that. Would you like to go to L.A.?"

"No." Why would he? There were too many people here.

Martha hacked an onion with trembling hands. "I wouldn't either. I like it here. I never wanted to go anywhere else. Just get married and raise kids like Mama and Daddy." Her smile faded a bit. "It's funny how life turns out, isn't it? Growing up, all the girls said I'd be married first, 'cause I couldn't do nothing else, and now . . . well, for Heaven's sake, Lucy's having a baby, and I'm paying my own bills teaching everybody else's kids. You know?"

*A baby?*

Dave's stomach tightened and he looked away, trying to sound casual as he asked, "Is she happy? With him?"

Martha's knife slowed. "She says she is." She glanced toward him. "That's not why you won't come into town anymore, is it? It's been five years now."

Five years in which they would have been happily married if his legs hadn't been crushed. Dave shifted. "No. I hardly think of her anymore," he lied.

Martha's shoulders relaxed, and she turned to scrape the cuttings into a frying pan. "I felt badly it didn't work out between you, but at least you hadn't married yet. It couldn't have been real love on her part."

Dave drove the knife through the thickest part of a carrot. If he'd married Lucy before he'd left, she'd have felt obligated to stay around long enough to realize he was the same person trapped inside a mangled body.

"Yeah?" he asked. "So tell me. What would *real* love have done?" The words felt so stupid. Like some people were destined to be together in some sort of blissful marriage that didn't exist, except in minds of girls like Martha.

"Well." Martha swallowed and wiped at tears from the onion. "If she had loved you, it wouldn't matter that you couldn't walk anymore. She would have stayed." Martha kept talking, even though he wished that he'd never asked. "You're not that different, you know? Just because you can't walk." Martha blundered on, stirring so fast that a potato leaped over the side of the pan.

Dave watched it thud onto the ground and slide a short, greasy path near her shoe.

"She could have helped you. You and Trey both, I mean." Martha prattled on, heedless of the escapee. "You've done a wonderful job on your own, but if you were married, Trey could be a boy and you wouldn't be alone all day. A girl would be lucky, you know, to have a husband who works from his own home." She tucked her chin into her chest, mumbling, "It's her loss, really."

Dave set down his knife, rubbing his temples to chase away the chatter. "Why? She has a husband. She has a nice home, and now she's having a baby."

"She's not happy," Martha said. "She *says* she is, but she's not."

That shouldn't pang. He shouldn't care what Lucy was doing now. It served her right if she wasn't happy with the man she'd chosen just for a roof over her head. Dave could have made her happy even if he was crippled. He chewed the inside of his cheek, wishing he hadn't brought it up.

"It's sad, isn't it?" Martha banged the spoon against the pan and replaced the lid. "How lonely everybody is. I think everyone in this town is lonely, but nobody will admit it. I know I am."

Hence the reason she was cooking supper for a hermit.

Dave shrugged lightly. "Guess it's normal."

"It shouldn't be," she answered quickly. "I don't think people were meant to be alone. I hate that you are." Her voice fell to a serious sort of hesitancy that Dave wasn't sure he liked. "I hate the idea of you and Trey struggling so hard over here. I think you're brave to go on as if nothing happened to you. I'd be scared to stay alone all day if . . . well, never mind."

She grabbed a rag from the sink, running it over the counter. "I was thinking maybe we could set up a visiting day at your house. I could help you and Trey get ready for company. Everyone could come here so you wouldn't have to travel. Just a few people for a get-together."

"No," Dave answered quickly.

Martha turned to face him. "Oh, but it could be fun. I'd do it at my house, but if I did, I know you wouldn't come."

"I don't want to see anybody."

"Why not?"

"Because I don't want them to see me!"

"There's nothing wrong with you." Martha plastered both hands against her hips. "Why, if you took care of yourself, you'd even still be handsome. There I said it. Yes, handsome. Like you were in high school. You could still be just as popular."

"I don't care about popularity," Dave answered. "I don't want people coming over here. Trey and I are fine."

"Trey will be graduating soon." Martha's voice softened. "What if he decides he wants to go to college? You can't live here alone. You need someone's help whether you're willing to admit it or not, and if you keep pushing people away, there won't be anybody left."

Dave stabbed the tip of his knife into his mother's prized tabletop.

Martha huffed. "Dave, I don't want to upset you, but I'm concerned. People don't understand why you don't go into town. They're worried about Trey."

"Well, they shouldn't be," Dave snapped. "Trey's fine."

She stood. "That's just it! You've gotten so short-tempered since you came back. They're afraid you're hurting Trey!"

Dave stared. "I've never hurt Trey."

"I know that," she said. "If you invited people over occasionally, they would, too, but you won't. You won't! You hole yourself up here and make everything worse."

Dave shook his head. "I have never hurt my brother, and I never will. What?" He gestured toward the battered boy on the couch. "Are they saying that I did that to him?"

Martha swallowed. "Well, Mr. Barrie says it was a bully, and I believe him, but they were all wondering why Trey didn't show up at work today. I wouldn't be surprised if the sheriff comes out to check on him."

"The sheriff needs to track down Joe and Michael who did it to him!" Dave roared. "If I ever hit Trey, all he'd have to do is run into the other room."

"See?" Her arm flailed out. "You're doing it again! You're yelling. You yell all the time. I've come here three times to get my brownie pan back, and every single time, you're yelling. At the radio. At the wall. At Trey. Your language is filthy, and you shouldn't scold him the way you do. I know it's hard for you, but you're really only making it worse."

"You're making it worse." He glared. "You should go. We don't need supper."

She gave a skeptical laugh. "Well, even if you don't, Trey does. So you can sit there and pout and watch us eat."

Dave peeked toward the boy on the couch and winced. "I don't think he can eat much. He's busted up pretty bad."

Martha softened. "Well, we'll find something for him to get down. It wouldn't hurt to clean up this house a bit, too. If he can't see well, we can't have him tripping over anything."

She wasn't going to leave. She was going to make herself

at home right here. Dave wondered what she would tell the suspicious people in town tomorrow. He wheeled himself into another room, drawing in slow breaths. Wouldn't she just go?

She didn't. She stayed cooking something on the stove that smelled better than anything he'd had in years. Something he wasn't sure he'd be able to eat now that he'd insisted he wasn't interested in food. She even did the dishes while it cooked. Dave picked up a few things that he could reach, but Trey had a habit of throwing clothing and other articles in the most inconvenient places.

He glimpsed Martha hovering over the kid like a mother hen, coaxing Trey to sit up with a bowl of soup. Dang, it smelled good. Dave rolled toward the porch, searching for air that wasn't saturated with fried potatoes. But Trey had replaced the rotted board across the bottom and the sloppy repair caught the wheels, nearly dumping him onto the porch.

Pain shot through both legs at the jolt. He cursed, using his weight to try to reverse himself, but that only made the wheelchair rock like a marooned ship.

"Don't go out." Martha's voice slithered into his ear. "Supper's ready."

She pulled his chair backward until it banged over the ledge and sent jolts into his spine, but he caught the cry before it reached his lips. She was pushing him. He didn't even let Trey push him.

He gripped the armrest hard before reaching for the wheels. "I've got it."

"I know," Martha said, but she didn't stop until he was at the table.

His eyes slid sideways. "Is Trey coming?"

"No. I let him eat in the living room."

It would just be the two of them at the meal. Dave swallowed, gritting his teeth. If he chased her off now, she would tell the town they were right and he was a monster. He'd have to delve deep to find the boy who had skated through life, always confident and polite. He begrudgingly dropped the napkin into his lap. Just eat and maybe she'd go home.

"Would you like to say grace?" Martha asked.

Dave's heart throbbed. The last time he had prayed, he'd begged God to not let them saw off his legs. He'd forgotten to request that they would heal. He swallowed, closing his eyes only long enough for her to follow suit. Then he studied her as he racked his brain for a prayer.

Desperate, he looked toward his mother's picture, then recited, "For what we are about to receive, let us be truly thankful."

Martha approved with a nod, and Dave wondered why. The sentence wasn't even addressing God. It was more of a suggestion to the rest of the people at the table, but once he actually tasted the potatoes, he truly was thankful.

He'd forgotten food tasted this good. Trey hated cooking, and the burgers he brought home from the diner were always cold before they reached the house.

"It's good," he offered so softly that he doubted she could even hear it.

Martha perked, sitting a bit straighter. "I think home economics in high school was the best thing that ever happened to me. My friends always said my cooking tasted worse than the cafeteria. Do you remember?"

Dave nodded. "I mostly brought my meals."

"I wish I could have." She brought a dainty forkful to her mouth and chewed before speaking again. "My mother hated cooking. She was terrible at it. Was your mother a good cook?"

Dave nodded. "I guess."

Martha giggled. "You probably don't remember. You never tasted the food. You always shoveled it in." She blushed and shrugged. "I used to watch in the cafeteria."

"I liked having extra time to visit," Dave explained. Make his rounds. Check out the girls. Monitor the guys. Nearly everyone at school had liked him. He was able to choose his friends. Martha hadn't been one of them. "You sat with Luke, didn't you?"

"Yes. Luke helped walk me through the town when I first came. He was a good boy. It's too bad he was killed."

Dave shoveled in another mouthful so he didn't have to answer.

Martha studied him before asking lightly as if the answer didn't really matter. "Did you see Luke? Once you joined the army, I mean."

Dave nodded, wondering why she'd put knives out for a meal that didn't need them. When she continued waiting for an answer, he said, "We were in boot camp together."

"What about after you shipped out?"

"Only a few times. We were in different platoons." He shoved the bowl toward the pot and helped himself to seconds, more interested in eating than discussing the mystery of what had happened to Luke Barrie.

"So you don't know what happened to him?" Martha stirred sugar in her tea, clinking the spoon against the glass. "When did you last see him?"

"Shortly before he disappeared." Dave's teeth clenched.

"You didn't see what happened to him though?"

Dave's fingers tightened on his fork. "When Luke disappeared, I was trapped under a collapsed wall. There were bombs and tanks everywhere, and, for all I know, he was blown to bits. Can we talk about something else?"

Martha winced as she folded her napkin and set it back on the table. "I'm sorry. I shouldn't have brought it up."

Dave fingered his temples as she rose and moved to the sink. "You liked him, didn't you?" he asked.

Martha hesitated. "Yes, though I'm not sure I was in love with him."

The sun cast a halo around her hair before she moved and the rays blinded him. Dave rolled back from the table. "You went to the dance with him," he said.

Martha collected the plates to carry to the sink. "That's because the person I really wanted to go with didn't ask me."

Dave glanced toward the table so he didn't have to look at her. "How was Trey when you woke him?"

She smiled softly as she wiped the table. "Oh, he was concerned about his face. He said he was going to look like a circus freak."

"He does."

"Dave!" She tossed a dishrag at him. "Don't say that. He'll be fine. Boys get into fights. They heal."

Dave frowned. Even things that healed still left scars, but it was too late. If Trey's face was scarred, he'd just have to get over it. "I wonder how long until his eyes heal well enough for him to go to school." He reached for the glass to finish off the last of the water. "I don't want him getting too far behind."

"I don't know." Martha dried the dishes and stacked them in a cupboard well out of Dave's reach. "Is he hanging out with that Howard girl?"

"They know each other. I don't know how much they're hanging out."

She stilled, looking out of the window. "I'm worried about that. She's strange, Dave."

She was bossy and forward, perhaps. Dave nearly grinned at the memory before he asked, "Strange how?"

Martha shut the cupboard. "She was talking to the graves in the cemetery."

Dave blinked. "She know somebody out there?"

"She doesn't know a blessed soul in there. She's just . . . Well, Trey needs to be careful. She's not from around here. We really don't know anything about her. I'm suspecting she's not even telling the truth."

"Her grandfather knows her. He wouldn't lie. He's a man of the church, isn't he?"

"Yes, but it's just strange. He never mentioned having a granddaughter, and now she shows up out of nowhere. She's a headstrong, stubborn little thing. Trey needs to be careful. I'd hate to see her getting him into trouble."

"They're kids."

Martha took a breath. "I know it's none of my business, but you are in charge of Trey now. Just make sure you know what he's doing. He's not really a kid anymore."

He stared. "What do you think Delilah's going to do, seduce him?"

Martha flushed, wringing the rag in her hand. "Her name's Delilah?"

"Yes."

She said it was Lila."

"Same thing."

Martha hung the towel on the back of a chair to dry. "Still, she could have said something."

"Why? I introduce myself as Dave. No one has a problem with it."

"Everyone knows your real name."

"Well, maybe she doesn't like her real name."

"Actually, I like my real name very much. I always have." Dave jumped as Lila's voice came from the front door. The screen creaked shut behind her as she strolled in as casually as if she lived there. "I was just told others wouldn't, and I'd be better accepted in this town if I went by Lila."

Martha sputtered as her cheeks flushed. "I didn't mean—"

"It's okay." Lila stuck out her hand. "I'm Delilah. You must be Dave's other tormentor."

Martha fumbled weakly with her hands. "I came to check on Trey."

"Really?" Lila smiled. "So did I." Her eyes swept the table. "Only I didn't bring peace offerings of food. Well, okay. I'm going to go talk to Trey. You two have fun in here." Her eyebrows rose and fell once toward Dave before she sashayed to the living room.

Martha swayed. "I'm going to go home, I guess." She gathered her brownie pan and moved for the door. "It was nice, Dave. I'll see you later."

Dave raised his hand in half a wave. With any luck, she would get busy now that her curiosity about their house and lives was satisfied. Lila's laugh and Trey's low voice carried from the living room. Dave set his jaw and rolled toward his bedroom. They were just kids. They'd be fine.

# 7

By the time Sunday morning rolled around, Trey's dignity was restored, and his face had healed into slight patches of discoloration. Trey growled as the house itself seemed to conspire to keep him from Lila's pew. His clothing wasn't clean. Dave whined as he left. Even the door stuck.

Trey brushed off the guilt as he kicked the screen into submission and hopped onto his bike. By the time he reached the church, organ music floated down the steps, accompanied by the voices of the punctual faithful.

Trey skidded to a stop and leaned his bike against the side of the building, wondering if he could see Lila from the clear glass in the round windows above the stained-glass rectangles. After a bit of wobbling on his delicately balanced bike, he located her sitting dutifully on the front pew peering at the ceiling while every other head bowed in prayer.

Lila jumped when she saw him, then rolled her eyes and mouthed, "What are you doing?"

"I'm late," he whispered back. He gestured helplessly.

Lila's eyebrows drew in confusion. She glanced toward her grandfather before slipping down the aisle toward the back door. Trey jumped down from the side of the building and met her on the porch.

"Trey, what in the world?" she asked.

"I was coming to church, but I didn't want to interrupt." Trey glanced over her shoulder. "Can people go in after it starts?"

"I don't know, but there's no reason to interrupt again," Lila answered. Her arm brushed his as she loped down the steps. "Let's go to the river."

"Won't your grandfather be mad?"

"He won't be able to come after me for a whole hour." Lila tugged on his hand. "We'll have plenty of time to make our escape."

Trey wasn't so sure about the idea, but he followed her down the steps onto Walnut Road. The breeze washed all thoughts of fire and brimstone away when he broke into a sprint, calling, "Race you!"

Lila caught up to him, and he grinned even when his lungs began to burn. Her hair escaped from her ponytail long before they reached the banks. When she bent to unlace her gray shoes, he wondered why she wasn't wearing the saddle shoes.

Before he could ask, Lila jumped straight into the water. Maybe her clothes were outdated, but they didn't look too bad once they were wet and had lost their boxy shape, clinging delicately to the very curves they were meant to hide.

She turned to splash him. "Are you coming in?"

Half a grin played across his face as Trey glanced around for any other heathens that might be out. Unlike Lila, he really couldn't afford to ruin his Sunday clothes. He kicked off his shoes and stepped into the water, wincing as the current pulled at his pants legs.

Lila disappeared underwater and reemerged like a mermaid with water droplets sparkling in her hair. She wiped her eyes, then grinned at him. "What's wrong?"

Trey winced, then shrugged. "I only have one pair of Sunday clothes."

Her eyes widened, and she shook her head as if it should be obvious. "So take them off."

His jaw dropped. "No, that's—"

Her grandfather would kill him if he was caught swimming with her in his boxers. So would Dave for that matter.

Besides, there was no manly way to admit the scrawniness of his legs, so he cannon-balled, clothes and all, near enough to splash her.

Lila laughed and kicked her way over to him, apparently forgetting that she had once claimed that she didn't know how to swim. "So, what do you know about baking?"

Trey's eyebrows knitted. "Baking? Not much, why?"

"I want to learn."

"Cool." Trey wondered if she knew that he only cooked for a living to avoid starvation. "What do you want to bake?"

"I don't know." Lila dipped her head back and floated with help from several air bubbles in her dress. "I've never cooked anything in my life."

"Why start now?" Trey swam to catch up with her in the stream.

Lila's face darkened. "My grandmother says I don't know anything a proper girl should, and she's right. I don't." She treaded the water, gently kicking her legs to keep afloat. "I want to show them I can take care of myself. I just have to learn how."

"Why don't you ask your grandma to show you?" Trey asked.

"I don't want their help." Lila's voice hardened.

"Why not?"

"I don't trust them."

"Do you trust me?" Trey moved a floating leaf from her path, keeping busy so he didn't have to look directly at her face.

"Yeah." Lila smiled slightly. "I do."

Trey swallowed. Lila had lied to so many people. Stories flowed from her tongue like water. How did he know which parts to believe? "So, when you said that—"

"Hey!" A gruff voice shouted from the shore. Old Mr. Carter waved a shotgun, running toward the fence that butted up against the riverbank. "Hey, kids! Get out of there! How many times do I got to tell you to stay off my property?"

Mud sucked at Trey's feet as he towed Lila out of the water. "Run!"

Barefoot, they scrambled up the slope of the river.

"What?" Lila screamed. "What's wrong? Why are we running?"

A gunshot answered her.

Trey struggled to keep up as his pants clung to his legs, gathering dirt and leaves. Lila galloped ahead until she slipped, slamming into the ground.

Trey grabbed her hand to jerk her up, but she motioned him down. "Stay here! He won't see us! Who the heck was that?"

"It's Mr. Carter," Trey huffed. "He's an old widower. His son died in the war, and he's been meaner than a wet hornet ever since. We must have floated too far down."

They held their breaths, but the woods remained quiet.

Lila sat up, peeling wet leaves from her dress. "He should be in church. He shouldn't be shooting at us. Idiot."

Trey's heart pounded. How would they get back to their shoes? They'd have to walk the long way around.

Lila giggled.

"What are you laughing at?" Trey demanded.

"You!" She shook her head. "You look so funny. Do you

realize we're running from a little old man? We must have looked so idiotic scrambling up the bank like that."

"A little old man trying to kill us!"

"Nah." Lila stood. "He wasn't that close to hitting us. He was probably just shooting to see us run."

Trey gritted his teeth as he pushed himself to his feet.

Lila caught up with him, reaching for his arm. "Oh, come on. It's over. No harm was done. We even ended up somewhere nice."

"We're soaked and shoeless and someone just shot at us."

"It'll make a good story." Lila laughed and worked her arms over his shoulders, nudging against him. "We could dance here."

Lila's arms warmed his skin. They were in a clearing, surrounded by an audience of smooth birch trees. He smiled, resting a hand on the curve of her waist. They danced slowly. No high lifts. No quick steps. Just two kids swaying without any music, except the bird songs overhead.

Lila's face changed from mischievous to soft and dreamy before her mouth turned down. Before Trey could fully analyze those emotions, she laid her cheek on his shoulder, and he forgot to worry about what she was thinking. He forgot that bullies had tormented him. He forgot that studies were tough. He forgot that his older brother couldn't walk.

Lila leaned against him, and he worried she would feel his heart pounding. He swallowed, then asked, "If I can get a car, do you want to go dance somewhere?"

Lila pulled back, studying his face. "'Somewhere' as in?"

"Breeze City has a real dance hall." Trey brushed a stray tendril of her hair from her shoulder. "We could go there."

She grinned. "My, my, I think I've corrupted you."

Maybe she had, but it didn't matter. Trey raised his eyebrows. "So, Friday night?"

Lila nodded. "Sounds good. My grandfather will be working on his sermon, and Grandmother will be out visiting. What about your brother?"

"What about him? He's a grown man. He can take care of himself."

"Okay. We'll see what we can do." Lila stepped back and glanced down at her sticky clothing. "I'm tired of being wet."

"We could go to your house so you can change," Trey said.

Lila shook her head. "No. If I do that, I'll be stuck at home. Can we go to your house? I'll just have to dry."

"My mother's dresses are there," Trey suggested. "Maybe you could fit into one of them."

Any other girl would be repulsed at the idea, but she didn't seem to be bothered by death. Lila nodded. "Okay."

Trey grinned. "And then we could continue dancing in the barn."

She pulled a wet string of hair away from her face. "Trey? What are you going to do after you graduate?"

"I don't know. Work at the Soda Shoppe full-time, I guess."

"Wouldn't it be cool if we became real dance partners? We could travel around and compete." Lila took his hand, then spun to walk in front of him. "We could go to New York! Wouldn't you like to see New York? I've always wanted to go."

Trey's eyebrows drew. "You said you were there when your parents died."

"And then I told you my parents didn't actually die. Not my dad anyway."

"How'd your mom really die?" Trey asked.

She flinched. "I don't know what happened to her. She disappeared. I never saw her leave."

"Why would she just leave?"

Lila walked a little faster. "If I find her, I'll be sure and ask."

Trey jogged three steps to catch up. "Hey. I didn't mean to upset you."

"Well, then don't talk about my parents, okay?" She spun, folding her arms across her stomach. "They both left me."

"At the orphanage?"

Her eyes rolled behind tears. "Something like that. Now let's go dance."

"Do you think your grandparents will be mad?"

"Oh, hang my grandparents!" Lila snapped. "Hang this whole town!"

Trey stuck his hands in his pockets and stayed quiet until they reached the farm. Lila hid in the barn, and he sneaked inside the living room.

Dave's eyebrows rose as he eyed Trey's soaked clothing. "What happened? They baptize you?"

Trey answered with a sheepish grin. Smuggling one of his mother's dresses to the barn was tricky, and he waited until Dave was fully engrossed in knobs and wires to sneak them through the living room.

Before he reached the door, Dave said, "I thought we could work on that car today."

"Oh, um, yeah. That would be good." Trey shifted, hoping the bulge under his shirt didn't show too much. "You mean right now?"

"Yeah."

Trey's mind raced. "Well, don't you . . . Shouldn't you finish that radio first?"

"I can do it later."

"Isn't that Mrs. Macy's?"

"Yeah."

Trey shifted in place. "Well, she was wishing she had it. Why don't you finish it first, and then we can work on the car? We don't want to keep her waiting."

Dave hesitated, eyeing the radio box. "I guess. Want to keep me company?"

"Well, I have . . ." Trey's mind worked to find an explanation. "It's just . . ."

"Okay, you know what? Just go. I get it." Dave waved him off.

Trey backed toward the door and freedom, offering, "We'll work on it tonight, okay?" He felt guilty for leaving his brother, but Dave could have friends too, if he wanted. Trey repeated that fact all the way to the barn. "Hey, Lila? I have a dress. Sorry it's old."

"Older than this one?" She asked from the hayloft. She slid down the ladder. "It's dry. It's perfect." She snatched the gown from his hands, disappearing into the tack room.

Trey stuffed his hands into his pockets again, walking in a large circle and doing a few spins until she emerged.

"It's a little big," Lila said, spreading her arms. His mother's blue dress made her eyes look an even deeper brown. She was gorgeous.

"It's fine," he murmured.

Lila swayed slightly, then gave him a tight-lipped smile. "Okay. We came to dance, not to stare."

Trey took her hand, pulling her close. He didn't want the lively songs and wild steps. He wanted to hold her. He wondered if he could get away with kissing her.

Lila cocked an eyebrow at him. "You look like you're contemplating eating me."

"I'm . . no, I'm . . ." Trey missed a step and landed on her foot. "Sorry. Sorry, no. I wasn't thinking about you," he lied, "I was thinking about Dave."

"You want to eat Dave?" Lila quirked an eyebrow and giggled before glancing back toward the doors. "Is he still in the house?"

"Yeah."

"What does he do all day?"

Trey shrugged. "I don't know. He pretends to work on radios."

"I thought he fixed them."

"Every once in a while he gets one working. Honestly, he's not that good. All of his skills are physical."

The song ended, and Lila dropped Trey's hand to scramble up the loft ladder. "You should put a swing in here."

"We have one outside," Trey answered.

Lila sat in the loft door, dangling her feet. "So, what's going on with Dave and Martha?"

"I dunno." Trey joined her, peering over the edge. "She keeps coming over. He doesn't want to talk to anyone."

"I don't blame him really." Lila's eyes darkened. "People are too snoopy. Too judgmental."

Trey shifted. "If you don't want them watching, why do you act so . . . different?"

Lila's eyes slit. "I figure they're already going to say nasty things, so I might as well laugh at them while they're doing it."

Trey leaned against the window frame, glancing over the fields. "So tell me who you really are."

Lila shifted, pulling her legs to her chest. "I can't."

"Why not?"

"Because you won't understand it."

"Try me." Trey reached for her hand. "No matter what you say, it won't change anything."

Lila didn't pull away, though she stiffened at his touch. "You say that now."

"Just tell me," Trey whispered, squeezing her fingers.

Lila huffed a laugh as her eyes misted. "I have a long history of being abandoned. I'd rather not add you to that list."

Trey cocked his head. "Because of the orphanage?"

Lila glared over the back fields. "The orphanage was the worst place I've ever been. I thought coming here would be better, but it's like being branded as a kid and no matter how hard they try to dress me up, they can't hide it. They say they love me, but they're trying to change everything about me."

Trey touched her cheek. "I wouldn't try to change you."

A small breath escaped, but she didn't look at him.

Finally, she said softly, "You might."

"Then tell me so I can prove I wouldn't." Trey scooted a little closer. "Come on. What could possibly be so bad?"

Lila lifted her face to catch sparkling tears.

Trey put an arm around her shoulder, pulling her into a hug. He'd held girls before sometimes, but he'd never had one cry on his shoulder. "Hey. Hey, it's okay. Whatever it is. It's okay."

Her fingers dug into his shoulder. "Trey, I can't tell you. I can't tell anybody."

"Why not?"

She shook her head. "Because you wouldn't understand."

"I'd try."

She was trembling, falling apart in his arms, clinging to him like he was the only thing keeping her grounded. "I can't."

They both jumped when the barn door opened, swinging sunbeams against them like a searchlight on a police chase.

Reverend Howard stood, arms akimbo, in the bottom of the barn. "I have been looking everywhere for you, Lila. Come down. We're going home."

He sent Trey a glare that made the boy imagine that the man was barring the gates of Heaven against him.

Trey stood as Lila moved toward the ladder.

Reverend Howard stared. "Where are your clothes?"

"I lost them in the river." She leaped from the last three rings of the ladder, landing with a solid plunk.

Reverend Howard sucked in a slow breath like he was praying in reverse. He glanced up toward Trey. "You two need to make sure you're with other people when you visit. Understand?"

"Yes, sir," Trey answered quickly.

Lila rolled her eyes behind Reverend Howard's back.

Trey remained standing until the door closed. He leaned against the ladder, feeling his legs shake. He wasn't used to incurring wrath from adults, but lately he couldn't seem to help it.

He kicked up dust, wondering if Lila would be grounded again. Then he glanced at the car. It was stupid to think he could get away with sneaking her to the next town for a dance without being caught. Why did her grandfather have to come along and spoil all the fun?

He pulled the tarp off his brother's car, surveying it. Dave had bought it with money saved from years of running a paper route. It was dirty and old, but it could clean up. If Dave got it running, Trey wouldn't have to take his bike. If he had a car, he could get into town faster and people like Joe would leave him alone. It was much cooler to have a car than a bike, even if the car was an old one.

He redirected his thoughts from girls to cars and returned to the house. "Hey, Dave! You want to work on that car now?"

Dave was parked at the window in the living room, but his eyes stayed on the last family portrait that hung crookedly on the wall. They'd taken it the day before he left for war. He'd missed the next Christmas, and the year after that, it was just the two boys.

"Trey, why do you keep bringing people here?" he asked.

"Because . . ." Oh, boy. Trey rolled his eyes. "I brought Lila here. Everybody else came on their own."

Dave rolled the chair to face him. "She left church this morning. Please tell me you had nothing to do with that."

"I didn't make her leave. I didn't even intend for her to leave. She just did." Trey plopped onto the chair, scraping the stuffing from a tear in the arm. "Dave, I don't get why you're so upset."

Dave spun his chair. "You were out in the barn with the reverend's granddaughter, and I had no idea what you two were doing out there. I didn't know what to say to him."

Why did every adult assume that two teenagers couldn't be alone for five minutes without getting into trouble? Either they had pristine youths or they'd gotten into trouble too, so who were they to talk?

"We weren't doing anything out there, Dave!" he snapped. "We were just talking. Did you know her grandfather doesn't allow her supper when she disobeys? Why is he acting like we're the criminals?"

"Trey, how he raises her is none of our business. She needs to start cooperating with her family, and you're getting in the way of that."

"Her family doesn't care about her! He has no idea who she is. He only wants her to be who he thinks she should be."

"They're trying, Trey. They're trying to help her become a functional adult."

"What do you know about functional adulthood?" Trey kicked a soda bottle from the coffee table as he propped his feet up and folded his arms over his chest.

Dave rubbed the wrinkles from his forehead.

"Trey, we're going to stop fighting and go work on that car," he said. "But you are not getting keys for it until you quit acting like a child."

Trey forced his hands to unclench. He could punch pillows later. He needed that car.

"Deal," he muttered, though he could barely manage to loosen his jaw.

—

Trey was no mechanic. Dave watched his brother work, wishing he could fix the engine himself. The boy knew nothing about cars, requiring explanations of where everything was located before he could be told what to do with it.

Maybe Martha was right. Maybe he had neglected his little brother too much. Trey wasn't prepared for life on his own. He needed to teach the boy how to drive. He had two years left with him. Two years and then . . .

Dave eyed the rusty nails loosening from the rotting walls. This barn wasn't going to last a few more years, but Trey's future wasn't in Graceland. He'd get the boy a car and find a way to pay for college. Then he'd deal with his own life.

He watched the sunset colors fading in the doorway, surprised at the clear memory of Lucy standing there in the red dress that had been her staple during the war. Her hair had been perfectly smooth, reflecting the golden flecks among the chestnut. He'd wished it was down and loose, remembering how softly those locks had slipped through his fingers.

"Dave?" she had asked.

The car stood between them, starkly reminding him that he would never drive it again. She had grown into a proper woman. He had degenerated into a helpless man. His eyes had slipped over her figure as her heels made soft clicks on the concrete floor.

She'd touched his shoulder, sending warm heat that both comforted and seared. It was maddening that he had to tug her down, silently begging her to consent to a kiss, instead of playfully stealing it as he had before.

She'd knelt in front of him, transferring her touch to his knees before quickly removing her hands.

"It doesn't hurt when you touch them." He'd reached out to catch her hand, thinking even if it did, the pain would be worth the pleasure.

She'd only squeezed his hand, then dropped hers to dangle at her side. "What happened?"

His heart had ached as though each beat was pushing the strength from his body. He hadn't wanted to think about watching the blood drain from the man who had planned to shoot him or the vague memories of the jostling journey to safety. He hadn't wanted to remember the pain of the festering wounds as they were cleaned and sewn without an anesthetic, or the way that the doctor's detached eyes had already roved to the next patient as he informed Dave that his legs would never bear his weight again.

He'd told her. She was still the only person who had heard the truth. His present mind begged his past self to keep his mouth shut. Even then, he had realized his mistake, backpedaling as her eyes turned from pity into anger that mixed with disgust.

"You left your squad?" she'd asked.

He'd winced. "I wasn't planning on running. I probably would have come to my senses and gone back. I wasn't thinking straight."

"No, you weren't." She'd pulled away from him, pacing to pet the horse in the opposite stall.

Dave couldn't turn away so he closed his eyes. "I know I shouldn't have run. But they'd just blown my buddy's head off, and I—"

"You have to tell them, Dave."

"I can't, Lucy. I wasn't supposed to be there."

She'd spun, startling the horse who backed away. "No, you weren't, and it wouldn't have happened if you had manned up and obeyed orders! But you didn't, so you have to tell them."

"I'd be dead if I had obeyed orders!" Dave had gripped the armrest. "You don't know what it's like to be surrounded by people trying to kill you."

Lucy's hands had flailed. "I understand why you ran. But you can't keep a secret like that! I never took you for a coward, Dave. This isn't like you."

"That's because it isn't me!" He'd groaned, rubbing one eye. "I lost my head. I panicked."

"You're not even listening," she'd whispered. She'd turned to a horse, working out knots in its mane. After a moment, she'd asked, "Why didn't you warn us about your legs?"

His face had flushed as his eyes dropped to the deformed limbs hiding beneath lumpy jeans. How could he explain that he still hadn't accepted this? That he kept feeling like it was a nightmare he would wake from? "I didn't know how."

"How?" She'd gripped the stable door where the horse had chewed through the wood. "Through a letter, Dave. Through a telegram. You write, 'Dearest Lucy. My legs were badly wounded. I may never walk again. Dave.'"

"I wanted to walk home."

"Well, you didn't!" Her voice had quivered. "I wrote you again and again and again, and you never wrote back. Not once for weeks. I thought you'd gone missing and no one knew, or you were grieving for your parents. So I wrote even more letters to help you through it, and you didn't even bother to let me know you were alive."

He'd tried to move toward her, first shifting in his chair

before remembering to roll it forward, but she'd stepped away from his advance.

"Lucy, I'm sorry. I didn't want you to see me like this."

She'd brought a hand up to catch her tears. "I don't care what you look like. I could live with that, but I can't handle this thing it's turned you into. Your mood. Your anger. Your excuses."

He'd clenched his teeth. "What do you want me to do! Things aren't like they were when I left, and I can't change that. I wouldn't have come back at all if I knew it would make you despise me."

She'd spun. "If you had earned that Purple Heart actually fighting, I wouldn't despise you."

He'd rubbed one eye, feeling his heart and face competing to burn the hottest. "Lucy. Please, don't—don't tell."

She'd sucked in a breath. "I won't tell, Dave. That's your job." She'd pressed her lips together, smearing red lipstick. "But I'm not coming back until you do."

She was blackmailing him into telling his secret? She may as well hold a gun to his head and demand he slit his own throat.

"Lucy," he'd whispered.

"I mean it, Dave."

"Get out," he'd hissed.

"Fine." Her words turned clipped and shrill. She'd wrested his ring from her finger, throwing it against the floorboards. It had bounced at his shoe, and by the time he looked up again, she was gone.

Now, with Trey bent over the hood, Dave allowed his eyes to rove the floor until he located the band. Even the diamond had dulled, blending with the tarnished gold against the wood. Dave snatched the monkey wrench, hurling it at the ring. It clanged, ricocheting its target into the darkest corner of the barn.

Trey jumped, banging his head against the hood. "Dang, Dave. What was that for?"

Shut up," Dave growled.

"Then quit throwing things." Trey stormed over to retrieve the wrench. "Why do you get so mad all the time?"

"You try staying in a chair all day, and we'll see what it does for your temper," Dave answered.

Trey's eyes widened slightly as he bent back under the hood, hissing like a leaking tire. "Try taking care of someone in a chair all day and see what it does for yours."

Dave shoved his wheels backward. "You know what? You can fix that car by yourself if you want it so bad."

"Fine!" Trey slammed the wrench onto the engine. "I don't need you!"

His phrase repeated, joining the taunting chant of Dave's wheels as they spun over the gravel. *I don't need you. I don't need you. I don't need you.*

# 8

Trey heard Dave's bed creak just before the shout reverberated through the house. "No. No!" Moaning, he shoved back the covers and ran to his brother's room to flip on the light. Dave's legs anchored him to the bed as every other part of his body flailed. Trey stumbled forward, tripping on Dave's pants sprawled across the floor. "Dave, wake up."

Dave continued cursing in his sleep with such vehemence that Trey's heart still pounded as hard as it had the first time this had happened. He inched closer to the bed, calling louder. "Dave, you're dreaming!"

He shook his brother's shoulder once, then jumped backward. Dave's hand caught his arm, reversing his momentum in midair.

Trey jerked against the grip. "Dave. Wake up, it's me!"

Dave's eyes snapped open, then slit. His fist lashed out, catching Trey's shoulder.

"Dave, stop it!"

Trey pushed his brother's shoulders against the bed to pin him down until Dave grabbed his arm. Throwing his weight backward, Trey felt his shoulder wrench as he fell. His back slammed against the pine floorboard, and before he caught his breath, Dave landed on top of him. Trey yelped as Dave managed to pin one of his hands against the floor.

"Dave, stop! It's me!"

Terror seized him as the moon lit Dave's eyes, illuminating the glazed hatred. He thrashed, trying to knock his brother off-balance until Dave's knuckles slammed into his mouth.

"Dave, stop!"

On the second blow, this one hitting his eye, Trey shoved the heel of his freed hand into Dave's eye. As Dave howled, shifting his weight to shield his face, Trey wriggled free. "What's the matter with you?" He scrambled to his feet and kicked Dave's ribs.

Dave continued fisting imaginary foes on the floor, screaming profanities Trey had never heard before.

Trey doubled over, grabbing his hair as he backed into the doorway. "Stop it! Stop it!"

Dave's eyes lifted toward him, then slit.

Trey slammed the door between them, running down the hallway like his brother could actually chase him. He turned the lock of his own door and crawled into bed, stuffing his pillow against his ears to block out the feud.

"Stop it, stop it, stop it," he chanted into his mattress.

He didn't go back. Not after he'd cleaned up his damaged face. Not after he turned on the radio to fill every nook in his room.

Not even when Dave's racking sobs penetrated the barrier as he called, "Trey? Trey?"

He owed his brother nothing. *Nothing.*

—

The sky lightened, shade by inconspicuous shade, mocking Dave's efforts to rise. His head pounded from a combination of racing thoughts, suppressed tears, and what he suspected were new bruises.

He wasn't sure what had happened. One moment he was struggling to pull himself from the wall and fighting a German.

The next, he was home and his kid brother was bleeding, screaming from the doorway for him to stop.

His legs throbbed, reminding him that he would starve if Trey decided he wasn't worth coming after. Growling, Dave rocked his shoulders, trying to gain enough momentum to push against the floor. If he could roll onto his stomach, he might be able to drag himself somewhere or at least get his pillow from the bed. But he'd worn himself out, and he let his head fall back to the floor. Humiliation rippled a familiar path from his chest into his legs. He lay still before sweeping one arm beneath the bed.

His fingers hit the canvas bag and found the iron barrel, feeling both the warmth of reassurance and the coolness of finality. Martha was wrong that Trey would feel obligated to care for him instead of going to college.

They might criticize him for it. Trey would hate him for a while, but the boy would be free to live his own life. Their farm would be sold. People would eventually stop whispering about him and mind their own business. Lucy might finally feel like he'd done the honorable thing. Maybe then she would wish she had stayed, but he wouldn't know. He wouldn't know anything anymore. He wouldn't feel guilt, humiliation, or regret.

*Would he?*

That question haunted him. He'd imagined different scenarios leading to the final moment when he pulled the trigger. But what happened afterward? Would he really just stop existing? Was there some sort of afterlife? A Heaven? Hell? Coming back as an animal? Out of the options, nothingness seemed the most comforting. Even sacrificing himself to free his brother couldn't redeem him in any hereafter. He was a deserter who'd never been discovered. He deserved to be shot.

He withdrew his hand from the pistol as Trey's bedroom door opened and closed. His heart picked up. Would the kid come? Or would he be too scared he'd get walloped again? Trey had his good traits, but he was a wimp. Dave couldn't even scold him if he did leave without coming in, but a day lying on the floor, especially if he messed himself again, might drive him to use the gun months earlier than he had planned.

The water ran in the bathroom. Trey was taking his own sweet time. The kid had ignored his pleas last night. Dave should have called that he was sorry, while he was at it. If he apologized now, it would seem like a desperate attempt to get help.

He waited for ten minutes, feeling his heart lurch as Trey's footsteps neared the door. Relief played through the shame. There was no way to look collected and calm when he was sprawled in his boxers on the floor, but he tried not to look too pathetic as his brother stood over him. He winced, catching sight of Trey's purple eye and a broken lip. Had he done that?

Trey folded his arms, leaning against the door frame. "Are you sane yet?"

It stung, but Dave managed a nod.

"You ready to get off the floor?"

Why was Trey treating him like he was a toddler throwing a tantrum? He wasn't even sure how he had gotten onto the floor. Dave shifted slightly, aching from the fall and hours on the hard boards. "That would be nice."

"So ask me. Nicely. And say 'please.'"

Dave closed his eyes, willing the burning from his cheeks. "Trey, just help me."

Trey's arms crossed. "That's not asking."

Dave growled, glaring at the brat. "Trey, help me up!"

"And that's not nicely."

He would not beg. He would not grovel. It was bad enough that his brother had to help at all.

Trey turned toward the doorway. "I'm going to be late for school. I'll see you after work."

Work? He was going to work? He wouldn't be home until dinner.

Dave cursed as he rocked to lift himself as far as he could manage. "Trey, get back here!"

Trey ignored him, walking to the kitchen to pour dry cereal into a bowl.

Dave panted, watching the fan whirl above him. He grabbed the bedpost, dragging himself inch by inch, whimpering in pain. He'd get his own self up. Trey would come in, see him halfway in his chair, and help him. He wouldn't really leave. He was just—

The front door slammed.

Dave froze, feeling his entire body pulse with his slowing heartbeat. "Trey?"

He heard the kickstand snap into place.

"Trey, you're a jerk, you know it?" he shouted.

"Hmm. I wonder who I learned that from!" Trey's voice floated through the fluttering white curtains, accompanied by the cheerful song of a bird.

The wheels crunched against the driveway, and Dave listened helplessly as the sound faded. When his surroundings grew still, he did throw a fit like a two-year-old, bruising both hands against the floor. He cursed until his throat was raw before he turned his fists onto the softer source of his agony.

A cheerful voice invaded the room, cutting through his rage. "Sure. Hit your legs. That'll help."

Dave's head rolled toward the girl in the door. Lila. Should he be relieved or upset? He wasn't sure, and his gaze returned to the ceiling.

"I was looking for Trey." The boards vibrated as she stepped next to his head and spread her arms. "I guess he's not here."

"Nope." Dave kept his eyes on the ceiling. He was shirtless, covered only by his sleeping shorts that revealed his withered, pale appendages in all their deformed glory.

Lila knelt and slipped her hands beneath his shoulders, pushing as he struggled to sit up. "Are you trying to get into the bed or the chair?"

"Chair," he croaked. Though he wanted to go back to sleep, he couldn't stand the idea of being stranded in bed when Trey came home.

Lila moved to the dresser. "I suppose this is where you keep your clothes." She dug through the mess and tossed him a shirt with a smile. "Not that you're not handsome without them."

He ignored the teasing, struggling to button the shirt before she returned with pants. Having a teen girl help him with his pants wasn't the most pleasant thing in the world, but he gritted his teeth against the pain. Lila released his pants once they were on and retrieved the chair.

Dave reached to button them. "You're going to be late for school."

"I'm heartbroken."

A slight smile pulled at his mouth, despite throbbing legs and fatigue. Lila was funny, having aspects of personality that reminded him of himself.

She rolled the chair over. "So, how bad did you get onto Trey yesterday?"

Dave tilted his head as she stepped to wrap her arms around his chest. Between his pushing and her pulling, they dragged him into the chair.

He panted before answering, "Not too much. Were you forbidden to eat dinner?"

"On the contrary." She moved to pick up her schoolbooks. "My grandfather threatened to make me eat everything. He said that it would fatten me up, make me lose my figure, and thus not be an object of lust." She cocked an eyebrow. "Think it'll work?"

Dave huffed a laugh. "I think you're making up a bunch of hogwash."

Her grin widened. "Congratulations. You're the only person in this town who has caught on to that." She tucked the book underneath her arm. "Well, I guess I need to go. I'll come after school to pester you as soon as I can sneak away."

"Take your time," Dave replied. But when she reached the door, he picked at his pants as he mumbled, "Thanks."

—

Lila walked fast, frowning at her gray flats and hoping Trey had gotten her good pair when he retrieved his Sunday shoes from the river. It was probably good she'd stopped by the house to get the saddle shoes, even if she'd left without her objective.

She slipped into the school just before Principal Gordon made his appearance to close the gates on any stragglers. Trey was already in his seat as she slid into hers, but he refused to look at her, keeping one hand tucked over his far eye. Did he know that Dave had fallen?

Halfway through class, she scribbled a note. *You look like you missed supper. What's wrong?*

The other students may not like her, but they passed the note beneath the desks until it reached Trey.

He read it, hesitated, and crumpled the note. His bruises looked like they had gotten worse instead of better. Had he been beaten up again?

Lila sighed, wondering if she could coax him to tell her what had happened. Or maybe he was quiet because her grandfather scared him away.

When the bell rang, she shot out of her seat to catch up with Trey. "So, what? Are you not talking to me anymore?"

"Huh?" Trey jumped, then shrugged, scuffing his shoes across the tiled floor. "No. I was just thinking."

About what?"

"Nothing." He shook his head, then sighed. "Dave and I fought this morning."

Lila winced. "Is that where you got the black eye?"

Trey flushed. "Yeah. No. Sort of. He hit me last night, but he didn't mean to. He was dreaming. Then I think he woke, but I don't know. It's like his brain doesn't wake up, so he doesn't know it's you."

"Who did he think you were?"

"I don't know." Trey palmed the back of his head. "He wouldn't stop. He wouldn't respond. So I just went back to bed."

Lila traced the binding on her book. "So, what was he like this morning?"

Trey flinched. "He was his normal grumpy self."

She blinked. "Did he know that he hurt you?"

"I don't see how he couldn't, but he didn't say anything. He just demanded that I get him off the floor. He fell last night while he was trying to kill me."

Lila couldn't tell if he was exaggerating or not. "Is he still on the floor?"

"Yeah. I wasn't going to get near him again." Trey spun the combinations to his locker with jerking movements. His voice wavered. "It was his own fault. He wouldn't ask me to help him, and I decided I won't unless he does."

"Well, at that rate, he's going to be on the floor for a week."

"Then he shouldn't be so stubborn."

"Still." Lila winced. "He could have fractured something. And he can't stay on the floor all day."

"I was thinking of checking on him at lunch," Trey muttered. "Maybe he won't be so stubborn then."

"Maybe." Lila watched Trey's face change as she spoke. "He is stubborn, but even if he's acting like a jerk, he can't get to water, and it's so hot today. "

Trey winced. "I said I was going at lunch! He'll survive a few hours."

Lila pursed her lips. "By the time you get home, it will have been over four hours, plus however long he laid there last night. He'll probably be too weak and sore to help you lift him."

Trey stopped now. "It's not that long." He blinked. "Well, actually, I think it was about midnight."

"Well, then it'll be about twelve hours before you're home if you go at lunch, and you won't have time to get there and back," Lila said.

Trey moaned. "Man. I didn't think about that." He swallowed, glancing toward the classroom doors ahead. Then he spun and walked toward the exit.

Maybe she'd taken it just a bit too far. Lila hurried to pull on his arm. "Where are you going?"

"I have to get him."

"You can't. You'll be in trouble for cutting class."

"I have to." He spun on her, and for a moment, he looked like he might cry.

She grabbed his shoulders. "Trey, relax. I already got him."

Trey's eyebrows scrunched. "What?"

"I stopped by to see if you found my shoes. He's in his chair now."

Anger flared through Trey's eyes, even as his chest collapsed in relief. "Why'd you act like—"

"Because life is no fun when you're on your own." Lila tugged him toward the class. "Come on. Let's just go to class."

—

Trey dreaded every turn of the bike wheel that brought him closer to Dave. What was he going to say? That he hadn't come back because he knew Lila had already been there? That he was sick of playing the father role while everyone treated him like a kid?

He never saw the boys behind the trees until they bolted toward him, bringing him skidding to a halt in front of his driveway.

Michael latched onto his bike handles as Joe yanked Trey from the seat, lifting him by his collar until his feet were off the ground.

Joe laughed. "Wow. His eye is black."

"Wonder how in the world that happened," Michael replied.

"Shut up and let me go," Trey snapped.

"I don't know. Should we make the other one match?"

Michael hurled Trey's bike against the tree. "Mrs. Melba already blabbed that we did." He smirked. "So who really did that, Trey? Your girlfriend?"

Trey wiggled, wondering if he could slip out of his shirt and make a run for it. If only he was taller. If only he was stronger. If only—

"Dave!" he called, though it was unlikely that Dave would be able to hear from the house.

The boy's hooted. "Dave! Dave, come quick! He's trapped! He's hurt! He needs you!"

"Dave!" Michael bellowed.

They waited, but the house remained still and silent.

"Hmm." Joe shrugged. "Guess he doesn't care." He hauled Trey into the woods.

Trey dragged his heels through the rotting leaves. Mr. Barrie's house was too far away for anyone to hear. No one else lived nearby. There was no way that he was going to get away until these boys were done with him.

Joe smirked as he pinned Trey against the ground.

"Dave!" Trey screamed. So what if it was cowardly and idiotic?

Joe reached into his pocket and pulled out a hot pepper. "Hungry?" He stuffed it into Trey's mouth. "Chew it, and swallow."

Trey spit it into his face. Joe picked up the pepper, snapped it in half, and rubbed the edges beneath Trey's eyes. Trails of fire burned their way into his skin.

He screamed as they howled with laughter.

"Next," Michael sang, holding his hand out for a second pepper.

The juice burned a path down Trey's throat as he swallowed the pepper just to get it out of his mouth.

A gunshot reverberated through the trees, sending the teen sprawling backward. Trey rolled onto his stomach, coughing up green flecks.

"Get out of here!" Dave barked. A second bullet skimmed the ground an inch from Joe's feet.

Joe scrambled backward, slamming against a tree trunk. "Son of a—"

Dave sent a third bullet to shave the bark from a tree near his head.

Joe howled, shoving Michael toward the road.

Trey struggled to sit up, though his eyes were too blurry to enjoy his rivals' terror. He held his face, hearing Dave's chair wheel snap a stick in half.

"Stupid kids, wasting my bullets." Dave sighed. "You okay?"

"Not really." Trey brushed himself off, blaming the tears on the hot peppers. He sniffed, sputtering, "I didn't know you could shoot that good."

Dave's eyes dropped to the pistol on his lap. "There's a lot that you don't know about me, Trey."

# 9

Trey turned the key and grinned as the engine roared. "Whoo!" He glanced toward Dave, who wagged his eyebrows. "Sure you don't want to come along?"

"Not with you driving!" Dave shook his head. "Remember, roads have rules. Don't drive it like you've been driving in that field!"

Trey grinned. He'd made some of his best memories these last few weeks, spending his evenings moving around imaginary stick-shifts as Dave described how driving felt in each gear. They'd go until the memory made Dave grumpy, and he'd quit talking about it.

As soon as the car sputtered to life, Dave made Trey drive in circles around his chair out in the pasture, yelling when to change gears. He sounded like their mother, cautioning Trey against every jostle, though it was hard to tell if he was more worried about his brother or the car.

"Come on. I'm ready. The road's going to be smooth as silk." Trey smiled at Dave, attempting to exude confidence and wishing Dave looked a little less like a kicked puppy.

"Don't hurt my baby." Dave caressed the chrome grill before he blew a slow breath. "Help me into the house, and then you can take it to school, but no driving over thirty."

Trey slid from the driver's seat and walked beside Dave's chair, only helping to push him up the ramp. "I need to get sunglasses."

Dave laughed, spinning the chair inside the doorway. "You couldn't pull them off. Sunglasses are for cool people like me."

"Yeah. You are pretty cool when you're not being stubborn." Trey backed down the steps with a grin. "Pretty cool. Not as cool as me."

He coaxed the car out of the barn and down the drive, hitting the asphalt without a backward glance. When he was out of sight—though not out of hearing range—he tested the engine, waving as he zoomed past William, who was picking tomatoes.

"Slow down, boy!" the man called.

Trey only grinned wider when he spied the owner of a certain pair of saddle shoes walking down the road ahead.

Lila surveyed him, slacking her weight onto one hip as he pulled alongside her. She cocked an eyebrow as she shifted her books. "I was going to ask where you've been lately, but I guess my question is answered."

Trey draped his arm across the seat. "Yeah. Get in, babe."

"Trey." Lila laughed before she tugged open the door. "That car is too old to get away with calling me 'babe.'"

Trey stepped on the accelerator. "But just listen to it."

Lila propped her feet on the dashboard, but a grin betrayed her. "Yeah, I hear that roar. Sounds like a dinosaur."

"It's a nineteen forty-two. It's not that old," he argued. "Dave was the coolest kid on the block when he bought it."

He detoured through Main Street, relishing the attention from the townspeople. He grinned when Lucy dropped a sack of groceries, feeling wickedly satisfied imagining Sheldon eating meals from produce that rolled over the sidewalk.

There was Dave's revenge. Now was his. He pulled his Chevy right next to Joe's prize in silent defiance of the broken bike. He didn't miss Michael's jealous glance before it was covered with a tacky remark about the rusted tires. It could be cleaned up. It could be painted and decked out. By the time school ended, Trey's notes were covered with drawings of a souped-up Chevy Deluxe, featuring upgrades he wasn't even sure existed.

"Hey, car-boy." Lila caught up with him on the front steps. "So are you taking me out dancing in that thing or aren't you?"

"Yeah, I'm taking you dancing." Trey glanced around, lowering his voice. "This week. I just have to figure out what to tell Dave."

"I have to figure out what to tell my grandfather. He's making me sit in the front row at church now. He said he'd call me out if I got up. I almost did anyway. He could tell me to stay, and I could tell him to . . ." Lila trailed off, tucking her hair behind her ear as she smiled at a passing teacher. "Anyway, I wouldn't have to obey. He can't make me."

Trey tried to listen, but his eyes hit the layer of mud crusted on his fender. He pulled a rag from his pocket, swirling a clean circle into the chrome.

Lila moaned. "Oh, you're going to turn into one of those boys."

"Don't worry." Trey patted the hood. "This is Dave's baby. You're mine."

She lifted her eyebrows. "Well, I should hope so. I don't play second fiddle to metal." She folded her hands daintily in front as she passed him. "Although I must say, Dave's not a bad-looking chap without his shirt."

Shock replaced every thought of a dirty fender. Trey clamped his hands over his ears, moaning as he doubled over. "Oh, my ears! You did not just say that!"

Lila opened the door, sliding onto the seat. "Say what? The part about him looking good without a shirt?"

Trey moved to put his hands on the car roof, leaning down until his face was next to hers. She sat so close he could kiss her if he had the guts. Neither moved and then he shrugged.

"Want to come help wash it?" he asked.

"You did not just say that!" Lila pushed him away. "Fine. Whatever it takes to go to the dance."

The dance. The one thing more exciting than owning a new car was using it to drive Lila to a dance. Conspiring to sneak away to Breeze City almost added to the excitement. By the time they reached the barn, they had a plan in place for Saturday night.

Trey killed the engine, sliding his legs out of the car and wondering if it was his imagination that they were just a tiny bit longer. "Come on. Dave's going to be waiting."

If nothing else, his brother would want to know that his baby got home safely.

"Trey?" They grinned at each other over the top of the car as Dave's voice carried across the yard. He sounded worried. Lila's giggle trailed away as the call came again, this time wobbling in pain.

"Dave?" Trey sprinted toward the house, but Lila reached the steps first. They split ways in the living room as she darted to the kitchen and he pounded to the bedroom. "Dave, where are you?"

"He's here!" Lila called before the back door slammed. "He's in the yard!"

The wheel of Dave's chair peeked over the porch. Dave clutched handfuls of grass, tangled beneath the bent metal like a snail with a shattered shell. Lila knelt next to his head, apparently unaffected by scraped skin and distorted bones.

Her hand flew out as Trey reached for the wheels. "No, don't move it! His legs are twisted."

Dave choked on strangled breaths.

Trey stumbled back. "I have to go to Mr. Barrie's. He has a telephone."

He left his girlfriend stroking his brother's hair and dove into the car, driving with the recklessness his brother had warned him against. He snaked across the entire road after the first curve. Slow down. Calm down. He was going to end up in a ditch like his father. Despite the warnings, his wheels skidded as he screeched into William's driveway.

"Mr. Barrie!" He left his keys in the ignition as he stumbled from the driver's seat, unsure whether to run to the barn or the house. "Mrs. Barrie!"

Laura rushed to the front porch with her hand pressed against her starched cotton dress. "Trey? What in Heaven's name?"

"Dave fell!" Trey gasped the words between breaths. "He fell off the porch, and he's all twisted up under the wheelchair."

"Oh, good Lord." Laura waved Trey inside, wiping the flour from her hands as she hurried to the telephone. The doctor's wife was on the party line, so it wouldn't be long before everyone in town knew that Dave had fallen.

Laura hung up before reaching for her handbag on the side table. "William's not here. He's taking the cows to Breeze City. We'll take your car."

Trey could not imagine the tiny woman driving any faster than thirty miles an hour, but he clung to the door handle as they skidded over the road to his house.

Lila met them in the driveway with a wet face and both hands raised. "He panicked and tried to shove the chair off. I couldn't get him to be still, so I pulled it free. His leg has a bad gash, but he won't let me get near him."

Laura slid from the seat. "He'll be all right. Trey, go inside and get clean cloths. We'll stop the bleeding. He'll calm down."

"He might hit you if he doesn't know it's you," Trey warned.

"He won't hit me," Laura said. She straightened her apron as she walked toward Dave who looked like he was losing the panic and nearing tears. Stooping beside the boy with her hands on her knees, Laura crooned, "Dave, can you hear me?"

Trey paused to watch his brother respond. Whatever memory that made him panic with Lila must be gone now because he wasn't shouting. A violent tremble had overtaken his body, but he opened his eyes. Whimpers bled through each breath, and the torment transferred itself to the elderly woman beside him.

Laura struggled to her knees, and Trey hoped Dave didn't start convulsing again. He held his breath as the woman touched the boy's face, releasing the tears. Trey backed up, turning toward the house. Dave's anger, he could handle. Dave bawling like a little kid was too much.

He grabbed a ratty towel from the bathroom cupboard before burrowing his face into it, resisting his own urge to cry. His stomach quivered, making him feel like he was a kid again, waiting for the train that brought his brother home.

He had lived with the Barries after his parents died, checking the mail every day for a letter from Dave. A month passed with no news, and when the Barries received the telegram that Luke was missing in action, Trey had cried as hard as Laura, terrified that Dave had gone missing as well. Two months later, a telegram addressed to Mr. Cunningham had arrived. Trey had trembled as he opened it, but inside was a simple message that stopped his tears.

*Coming home. Dave.*

He'd waited with the rest of the town, shifting from heel to toe as the train ground to a stop. Beside him, Lucy had clutched a white hanky that she dabbed against both her wet cheeks and colored lips. Trey rolled his eyes, but he'd had better things to worry about than his brother's girlfriend. He had every intention of reaching Dave before she even had a chance to spot him.

The crowd had cheered as the train pulled to a stop, letting out steam like an exhausted sigh. Neighbors pressed against Trey, and he'd tiptoed to see the passenger car as boys began swinging out of the door. Jimmy. Erik. Sylvester. They'd all been met with hurrahs from friends and smothered with hugs, kisses, and tears from mothers and girlfriends.

Lucy had bounced in her white heels. Trey frowned, wanting to be the first to hug his brother. Little brothers shouldn't come second to girlfriends, but he had a sneaking suspicion that he would be waiting for at least one kiss to finish before he could intervene.

Lucy was pretty. Dave wouldn't see Trey at all if he kept standing next to her. He'd shoved his way closer to the train as Jason jumped onto the platform. Then John.

Peter's mother had nearly trampled Trey on her way to her son. She'd clung to him in a way that the guy would once have found embarrassing, before asking, "Where's Sheldon?"

Peter had frowned. His eyes darkened, and his chin rose. He'd swallowed, glancing back toward the train. "He's helping Dave." Then his eyes had moved to Trey to give him a small smile. "Hi, kid. Good to see you."

Trey could hardly tore his eyes from the door. "Where's Dave?"

The crowd had quieted as Sheldon and Tim lifted a wheelchair onto the platform.

Lucy screamed.

Before Trey had recovered from the noise, she'd thrown herself at the chair, wrapping her arms around whoever was in it. Trey watched, feeling trapped in his own stiff body.

"What happened?" Peter's mother whispered.

"There was a bombing. A building crushed his legs." Peter had answered. "You didn't hear?"

William had clasped Trey's shoulder as the boy swayed. Trey shrugged it away. Dave's face was white and haggard, but when he'd saw Trey, he'd held out an arm. Trey had stumbled from William's hands to Dave's arm, finding the returned embrace weak, but stubborn.

Dave had set his face into Trey's shoulder and didn't lift it as voices around them hushed. "I missed you, kid," he'd whispered.

Trey's voice shook. "I missed you, too."

Dave had held him out at arm's length, forcing a shaky laugh. "Hey, look. You grew. I said you would."

"Yeah," Trey answered. He'd only grown an inch. Dave had shrunk several feet, putting them at eye level.

Dave had glanced behind Trey. "Where's Mom and Dad?"

Trey sputtered, choking out half syllables, but no one from the crowd stepped in to speak for him.

Panic crept into Dave's face. He'd gripped Trey's arms until they hurt. "Where are they?"

"They're dead." Trey's weak answer was the only thing heard on the station platform.

Several women's hankies went to their mouths as Dave stared. His chest heaved several times. "What?"

William's shadow had moved across Dave's face as the man steadied the boy's shoulders. "We tried to get ahold of you. It was an automobile accident."

Dave's head had begun to shake as soon as William spoke.

His whispering grew louder like he was trying to cover the words. "No, no, no."

The crowd had edged away. A few ventured closer, trying to offer condolences. Dave waved them away with profanities he'd never said before the war. Trey backed into Lucy, and she'd wrapped her arms around him as they watched the man writhe in the chair. Cursing God. Cursing the army. Cursing America. Trey had spent the next six years trying to forget the stunned expressions on people's faces.

"Trey! Where are those towels?" Lila rushed into the bathroom.

Trey hugged the towel to his chest, swaying away from her before he remembered what they were for. Lila's shoulders sank, but she took the cloth, wetting it without comment.

Trey swallowed and followed her back to the yard. Dave laid flat on his back now, with one leg still twisted. He must be hurt because he wasn't protesting Laura's touch or soothing words, though she smoothed his hair back like he was a toddler.

Trey took the towel from Lila, inching toward the pair on the grass. "I got the towel, but if I hurt him, he might panic. You need to move away."

The woman shook her head. "Dave's not going to panic, but even if he did, we'd forgive him."

It was easy for her to say. Dave hadn't tried to kill her yet. Trey knelt beside his brother, gently pressing the towel against the blood that seeped through the gash in Dave's pants until the doctor arrived. He backed away from the trio as Laura explained the situation, gritting his teeth every time Dave cried out while the doctor explored the mangled bone.

His stomach churned long before the doctor recruited him to help hold Dave as they set the leg. Trey squeezed his eyes shut, feeling his throat pump as he searched for any thought to distract him from his brother's pain. He found one. A wonderfully selfish thought. If Dave was in the hospital, Trey was a free man. Taking Lila to the dance was going to be a breeze.

# 10

I got you a present." The conspiracy in Lila's eyes was nearly gleeful as Trey met her in the alley next to the Soda Shoppe. She held out a box. "Open it. I've been waiting all day."

Trey grinned as he loosened the very girly bow. Inside the box lay black wing tip dress shoes. He pulled them out, feeling his heart pound in his throat. He should say something, but all he managed was a pathetic sputter. "I didn't bring you anything."

Lila laughed. "I figured Mrs. Mallary must have ordered those just for you. You know, before you blew your savings on mine."

Trey jolted, then grinned. "How did you know?"

"You kept looking at them, and you were there when Georgia so graciously pointed out my war rations." Lila motioned toward his feet. "Go ahead. See if they work."

Trey tugged on the shoes, finding an even bigger smile. "Guess tonight's a good night to break them in." His feet were going to blister within a few hours, but it would be worth it.

He reached for her hand, towing her toward the car. Lila settled herself into the seat as he dutifully drove from the town until they hit the country roads. Trey sped up as a lively song blared trumpets from the speaker.

"It's my song!" Lila laughed and turned up the volume to sing off-key with Donna and her men, "De-li-lah..."

Trey joined in the song just before the engine sputtered. He groaned. "I forgot gas."

"We can go back," Lila answered. The car coasted to the side of the road. "Or not . . ."

Trey groaned, setting his forehead on the steering wheel as the music continued extolling the virtues of being with Delilah. Dave would never have run out of gas on a date unless he planned on it. "We're miles from town. By the time we walk there and back, we'll miss the dance."

Lila climbed out, studying the cornfield. "We're not far from Mr. Barrie's house if we cut across the field. We could walk there and see if he has gas."

Trey nodded. "I suppose we don't have much of a choice."

Every step felt like an hour lost, but at least he was with Lila. He thought about holding her hand before deciding against it. They weren't really together. They weren't a couple. He wondered if she would be his girlfriend if he asked her.

By the time they reached William's farm, he was worried he'd completely ruin his new shoes before they ever touched a dance floor. Would William notice and ask about their attire? He was dressed for Sunday. Lila wore a suspiciously heavy coat that suggested she was hiding a doozy of a dress. He wasn't used to sneaking, breaking rules, or keeping secrets.

Lila had no such qualms. She bounded up the steps and knocked on the door, straining to listen. "Mrs. Barrie!"

Trey shifted at the foot of the stairs as no sound of life came from the house. The car was missing as well. "We could check the barn," Trey suggested. "Mr. Barrie might be in there."

Lila rubbed her arms as she tromped down the steps.

"They have to be there. I can't sneak out like this twice. It's today or never."

Trey held his breath as they stepped into the barn, but its only inhabitant was the old plow horse who nickered from the stall.

Trey laughed, gesturing. "We could take Chester."

Lila's eyes fixed in the far pasture showing through the barn door. "We could take the truck," she said.

"Mr. Barrie's work truck?" Trey asked.

"He's not using it."

Trey stared. "Lila, that's stealing."

"It's Delilah, and it's only stealing if we don't bring it back. It's so far out, and it'll be dark soon. He probably won't even realize it's gone."

Trey shook his head. "I don't know."

"Oh, come on. It's Mr. Barrie. Even if he finds out, he won't care. He'd let us take it if we asked. We could explain."

"I don't think Mr. Barrie would approve of us sneaking out to dance."

"Well . . ." Lila inched toward the truck, toying with her hair. "We could take it into town to get gas, fill up your car, and return it. If it's a work truck, he probably leaves his keys inside. If not, I'm sure we could find a screwdriver."

Trey jerked his head toward her. "You know how to start a car with a screwdriver?"

Lila hunched her shoulders, guiltily chewing one side of her lip. "Maybe."

"If the keys are inside, we'll take it. If not, we'll leave it alone," Trey answered. He swallowed, trailing her across the field to peer into the window. The key sat snugly in the ignition as if the Devil had left it on purpose.

"Keys are here!" Lila yanked open the door to climb into the passenger seat. She pulled them free and flourished them in the air, mimicking William's accent. "The dancing gods have smiled upon us!"

Trey took a breath. "Well, if we told Mr. Barrie we just needed gas, he wouldn't mind." He blew out a breath and climbed into the driver's seat and turned the key. The engine roared to life like it was as desperate for a night on the town as they were.

Lila bounced in the seat. "Come on. It's more interesting this way, isn't it? Years from now, you can tell your grandchildren all about the time that you stole Mr. Barrie's work truck for your first date."

Trey nearly banged his head, swinging into the cab. "You said it wasn't stealing!"

"It's not, but you always exaggerate stories to your grandchildren. Unless you're my grandpa. Then every story has a moral."

Trey wondered what moral Reverend Howard would attach to this particular tale. He inched onto the driveway toward the road, driving more gently with the old truck than he had with his own ride. "I don't know how much gas I can get. I only brought enough money for us to go to the dance and get something to drink."

"I don't have any." Lila winced. "All I had was birthday money, and I bought your shoes." She chewed a nail, eyeing the road in front of them. "We'll have to be careful too. My grandfather can't see us together in Mr. Barrie's truck—or anyone else, for that matter."

Trey swallowed. That was a good point. Getting busted was one thing. Getting busted before they even got to dance was another. They neared the crossroads. Left and back to town? Or right to the dance hall? Left? Right? Left? He turned right.

Lila laughed, shooting a fist into the air. "Whoo! He's becoming a rebel!"

Trey grinned to cover his pounding heart. "You're right. Mr. Barrie won't care."

Lila turned on the radio, cranking up the crackling speakers until the brass band blared. This date wasn't anything like Trey had imagined. Instead of cruising along with nice clothes and a sleek car, they were bumping around a rusted truck with air rushing in the windows and whipping Lila's hair around her face. She was giddy at their mischief, and he started laughing, too. There was something exhilarating in being bad.

In the slower truck, it was dinnertime before they reached Breeze City. They puttered into the parking lot, managing to distract even the couple kissing in the car next over.

"Come on, don't stare." Lila shoved open the door. "My dad always warned me to 'stay in the building.' We can't let him down, you know."

The precaution was well heeded. Lila stepped onto the parking lot, letting her gray coat drop to reveal a dress that hadn't come from her mother's closet or anywhere in her grandfather's house. A royal blue skirt swished around her knees, narrowing into a bodice that hugged every curve.

Trey stared, and so did every other guy in the parking lot. But it was his arm that she took. Sixteen years old, and he'd achieved his greatest moment of triumph.

This place was no Soda Shoppe. The floor was sleek, kept clear only for dancing. Tables were set around the walls for spectators. There was even a live orchestra.

Before he had time to really study the dancers or their moves, Lila grabbed Trey's hand and pulled him toward the floor. "Come on!"

Trey forgot about Dave, William's truck sitting like a turkey among peacocks, and everything else that had happened the last few days. It was Lila and her brown eyes. Her body swinging in and out of his arms. They were a team, and they were good. So good that they continued for three dances before stopping to breathe.

She laughed between gasps as she bounded off the dance floor as carefree as he'd ever seen her.

"I'm getting drinks." Trey winked. "I know, I know. You like root beer." His strut was a bit more confident than it ever had been. He'd ask her the question tonight. They could be officially dating in secret. He slid coins across the counter, exchanging them for a Coke and a root beer and reveling in being a customer for once.

His steps slowed only slightly when he saw Lila's mouth moving as she chatted with someone who was blocked by the crowd. He jolted when he saw the man. Dark hair slicked with pomade. Perfectly creased pants. His shoe propped onto the seat of Trey's chair, a lit cigarette dangling from the side of his mouth and several more tucked into the folds of his white sleeve. He looked like he'd stepped right down from the silver screen.

*Back off, buddy. She didn't come alone.*

Trey rehearsed the speech in his head, but before he could manage to say it, Lila spied him and waved him over.

"Trey! This is Darryl. Darryl, this is Trey from Graceland where I'm living now." She turned toward Trey, eyes sparkling. "Darryl and I grew up together." With the way the guy was looking at her, Trey wondered if that was all they had done, but he forced a smile and held out his hand. "Hi, Darryl."

Darryl's eyes slid slowly down him, and Trey straightened as tall as he could, wishing he was about two feet taller and six inches broader. Even when Darryl's eyebrow cocked, and he grinned behind his cigarette, Trey kept his hand stubbornly extended between them until Darryl clamped onto his hand.

"I haven't seen Delilah in years," Darryl said. "You won't mind if I steal her for a dance, for old time's sake?"

Yes, Trey minded. He minded very much. But when he turned to Lila, her eyes were hopeful.

*Drat.*

He shrugged. "No, that's fine."

It would be helpful if Lila didn't look quite so ecstatic.

Trey sat as the couple moved toward the dance floor. He slouched, pretending that he wasn't bothered by them holding hands, or the way that Darryl felt so free to put his hand on her waist, or how easily Lila followed the guy's lead. He couldn't even revel in his handiwork, seeing his pupil move that smoothly across the floor with another guy.

The dancers here were good. They were doing dances that he had never seen before. Darryl tossed Lila over his head like she was nothing, but Lila didn't seem worried or even fazed. She moved as though she had done this a thousand times. Darryl pulled out a second array of complex movements, and Lila went through like a trained horse.

Trey squirmed, feeling bile rise in his throat.

When the song ended and Lila's feet returned to earth, Darryl dropped a kiss on her cheek, whispering something. Then another girl cut between them, swaying in front of Darryl like an enchanted cobra until the guy took the bait. Lila laughed, shaking her head as she returned toward the table.

Trey stared at the ring around her root beer. She was his. He brought her. He taught her everything she knew.

She slid into the seat, reaching for her drink. "Gosh, I'm thirsty."

Trey tapped his Coke. "I didn't teach you to dance, did I?"

Lila's eyes flickered up, and the liquid froze in her straw before she released it. "Why do you say that?"

Trey's hand swung out toward the floor. "I didn't teach you half of those moves. Heck, I've never even seen half of those moves."

Lila shrugged lightly. "Darryl's a good dancer."

Trey shoved his chair backward. "Come on, Lila! I know you better than that. Quit lying!"

He needed air. He needed to get out of the building. He abandoned both Coke and girl and moved toward the exit. Lila could charm her own way home.

"Trey!" Lila ran after him, grabbing his arm. "What's eating you? You said you didn't care if I danced with him."

"Of course I said it." Trey's free arm flew out. "You wanted to dance with him! You weren't supposed to *believe* me."

"Oh geez, really?" Lila rolled her eyes, following as he shoved his way out the doors. "It was one dance! We're not even officially dating!"

"I don't think it would matter to you if we were," Trey spat, interrupting the kissing session of the couple still in the car next to him. "You don't care. You go wherever the breeze blows you. Do whatever you feel like doing—"

"Shut up!" Lila's eyes blazed. "Shut up, Trey!"

"Why? It's true."

"So?" Her arms flailed. "That's what my parents did. If you don't like me that way, you need to find another dance partner because it's the only way I know how to get through life!"

Trey huffed. They weren't going to dance again tonight, but he couldn't really leave her here. "Come on. Let's just stop talking and go home."

She shook her head, blinking rapidly as she glanced back toward the dance hall.

Trey grabbed her hand before she decided to find Darryl. "Come on. It'll be okay. Let's just go."

Lila jerked her hand away, glaring before she swept toward the car like he was just her chauffeur.

Trey yanked her door open. With luck, he could get her home, gas up his car, and return William's truck to the field with no one the wiser.

Lila rapped her knuckles against the window. It drove him crazy, but when he glanced over, he swore he saw tears. He was still mad. He wasn't ready to talk her into peace yet. He gripped the steering wheel until pain shot up his arms.

Lila bounced her leg as if fighting the urge to jump out of the car. "Just drop me off at the edge of town. I can find my own way home."

"I have to get gas."

"Aren't you afraid to be seen with me?" Sarcasm dripped through her voice. "Since I'm such a bad influence on you?"

"I'm not dropping you off at the edge of town." Trey spoke through gritted teeth. "You can walk home from the gas station if you insist, but I'll follow you right to your door."

"My gosh." She groaned. "I really have been a bad influence on you."

Trey turned up the music that sounded irritatingly happy. Lila scowled and punched it off. He'd have to hurry or the station would be closed by the time he got back. He pulled into the dim station closest to the edge of town, filled up a gas container in the back of the truck, then moved on. At least now he really was using William's truck for gas. They'd hardly done anything else.

He pulled up in front of Lila's grandfather's home, and the curtains next door parted as Mrs. Melba peered out. Lila didn't seem to care as she slid out and marched up the drive. Trey grumbled all the way to his car, filled the tank, and dropped off

William's truck. No one came to check on him, and he didn't stay, even though William and Laura had offered to let him sleep at their farm while Dave was gone. Dave would go to their house while his legs healed, once the doctor decided he was sane enough to be released.

Right now, Trey didn't want to see anyone. He stomped to his car without caring if his shoes were destroyed and drove like a madman back to their empty farm. Parking his car in the barn, he finished the tantrum by slamming his car door.

As he reached for the light switch, Lila's voice stilled his hand. "The only thing worse than having people mad at me is having them mad at me and not knowing why." Her head appeared over the hayloft. "So tell me what's wrong instead of just brewing. What do you want?"

Was she serious? He was mad because he liked her. He was mad because he couldn't date her. He was mad because she lied to him.

Trey glared. "I want you to tell me the truth!"

"The truth?" She sounded dazed, like that was something nobody had ever asked her to do. Her head disappeared, and rustling hay suggested that she had flopped into it. "The truth is that you're a good dancer. You are, for here, but there's a whole world outside of Graceland. They know newer dances that you've never seen. Out there, you're good, too, but you're not great. It's a bigger pool."

He hadn't expected an attack on his dancing skills, though her tone of voice was more subdued. Trey climbed the ladder to find Lila staring at the rafters. "So how come you didn't tell me you could dance?"

She shrugged. "You offered to teach me. I thought it was cute. I thought maybe you wouldn't dance with me if you found out I was better than you."

He flinched as he fell beside her, careful to keep his face from her view. "I don't get it. Who are you?"

"Delilah."

He ground his teeth. "And who is Darryl?"

Lila shook her head. "He lived by the orphanage. He used to sneak across the street and talk to me over the fence. He liked me because I was a charity case and nobody really cared where I was or when I got back."

"But you dated him?"

"He took me dancing a few times." She glanced over, raising her eyebrows. "We stayed in the building. The last time we went, he tried to kiss me, and I punched him."

Trey turned, squinting at her. "Are you telling the truth?"

"Yes, Trey!"

"So what else have you lied about?"

"To you?"

"Yes, to me."

"Not much." She shifted, drawing her knees to her chest. "I might not have lied to you at all if it wasn't for my grandparents. I would have told you my name was Delilah. I would have told you my father wasn't dead. I might have told you my mother ran off and left me. I would have told you the war ruined my life as much as it ruined Dave's."

Trey nested his hands behind his head. "Because it orphaned you? Was your dad a soldier?"

"No."

"What then?"

"I can't tell you."

"Why not?" Trey pressed. "I won't tell."

"You're better off not knowing."

He huffed. "Well, if you can't trust me, I don't know how we're going to make any kind of go of this."

Lila blew out a slow breath. "You have to promise never to breathe a word to anyone."

Trey tucked his hands behind his head, settling in the hay like his heart wasn't pounding. "I won't."

"And you can't get mad."

"Why would I get mad?"

"You can't, or I won't tell you."

"Fine."

Lila swallowed, but she didn't look at him as she blurted, "My real name is Delilah Schneider."

Trey sat up, feeling his heart pound in his ears. He turned his face toward the darkness beyond the barn. "Your dad's German?"

Lila picked straw from her dress as she spoke. "He came to America before the war began, but his family is still in Germany, except for Mom and me. He had a father and mother, four sisters, and two brothers who died during the war."

"They were Nazis?" The word tasted foul in his mouth.

"See?" Lila's hand batted the air between them. "You're already getting mad."

It was true, but Trey denied it. "No. No, I'm just asking."

"Yes, they were." She set her chin on her knees. "The first war crippled their country and destroyed their resources. It doesn't make what they did right, but they grew up without hope, and Hitler offered a chance to rebuild their lives."

"By destroying everyone?" Trey muttered.

"I'm not siding with them," Lila said. "Dad left Germany and came to America, but he's not a spy."

Trey's head began to throb. "Does your grandfather know?"

"I think so. Anyway, my father ran because someone found his correspondence with his brothers, and he was afraid they'd arrest him. He snuck back one night to see us, but he and Mom fought. When I woke up, she was gone, and he took me with him. We traveled a while before he left me at the orphanage. He sent two letters while I was there from two different states. Then he quit sending them at all." She knuckled her eyes. "So, now you know."

Trey took a slow breath, fighting the churning in his stomach. Her father wasn't a Nazi. Neither was she. He eased back onto the hay beside her. "And that's why your mom left?"

"I think. I don't know. I get why she left, but I don't know why she left me." Lila pressed her lips together. "I think Dad only left me because he was scared to keep me while the war was still going. He'll be back someday, and I'm going with him. I don't care what my grandparents think."

Trey shifted. What if her father really was a spy, and she just didn't know? He rolled onto his stomach, watching the fading daylight dimming the barnyard. "You won't always have to live with them. You can find a place to board here when you get older and help me run my dancing studio."

"You should turn the barn into a studio." Lila snagged the change of conversation. "You could bring in people that know different kinds of dancing. Swing. Ballet. Tap. All of it."

"In the barn?" Trey asked.

The idea stirred his imagination, destroying the image of Lila running off with her German father who wasn't a Nazi. Or being arrested for dating her and facing an official interrogation where they would decide he was a sympathizer.

"Um-hum," Lila continued, painting a much rosier future.

"Would you help me with it?" Trey asked.

"Um-hum."

Trey scooted a little closer, keeping his eyes on a light that was left on in the house. "Would you go steady with me?"

Silence. That wasn't good. Trey glanced over, prepared to

say he was just kidding, but Lila's eyes roved in thought like she was contemplating it. He wasn't sure he'd ever had a girl contemplate any offer from him.

"Have you ever had a girlfriend?" Lila asked.

"Um . . ." Trey squirmed. "Not really. Unless second grade counts."

She chuckled. "It doesn't."

"Then, no."

Lila lifted her chin from her knees. "Seeing how I just told you I'm the daughter of a German immigrant—after dancing with another guy—and you're still crazy enough to ask . . ." She smiled. "Sure. I'll be your girlfriend."

It wasn't the enthusiastic answer Trey was hoping for, but it would do.

Could he kiss her now, or would she punch him too? He'd never kissed before. He might botch it. Then again, how hard could it be?

Lila scooted away to perch on the edge of the loft, resurrecting her daydream by pointing to the roof beams. "You could rig up lights for the studio. If you sanded and coated the floor, it could clean up."

He could make money by dancing with Lila. His eyes wandered from beam to beam, trying to imagine that the glowing sunset was lights in the studio, and he was dancing with Lila.

He needed to take her home, but they would get back no later than if they had danced. When the sun set and a chill descended, he put his coat over her shoulders.

Her ideas lagged as her body stiffened, but she hugged his jacket close. He edged away like she was a wild animal who might bolt, focusing on the imaginary dance studio when all he really wanted to do was kiss her. He listened until her voice grew hazy, like a radio out of frequency, and it occurred to him what he had managed.

Delilah, the girl with no proper upbringing or manners, the little liar who snuck out of church to consort with heathens, was his. So maybe she was too scared to kiss him. She was wearing his jacket. She'd said she'd be his girl. He was the only person in town who knew the truth about Delilah Schneider.

When he opened his eyes again, the walls were splashed with pink and yellow. Trey jerked upright, staring at the sun that peeped over the fields.

How'd he get into the barn? He'd been talking to Lila and then—

"Lila?"

Trey scrambled to his feet, both hoping and fearing that she'd gone home on her own. But a bright blue dress betrayed her curled like a cat over by the loft door. Her hair had loosened and captured bits of hay and her mouth was parted the slightest bit, just begging to be kissed.

She'd look adorable if he wasn't so dead.

Trey shook her awake. "Lila? It's morning."

Her eyes fluttered open, and she squinted. "What?"

"We fell asleep. It's morning."

"Morning . . ." she mumbled before she jolted upward. "Shoot!" She twisted her body impossibly tight to glance out the window, then scrambled to her feet, brushing hay from her dress. "We stayed out all night. We're never going to see each other again."

"It's okay. We'll tell them the truth. We were talking, and we fell asleep."

Her arms flailed. "Yeah, like they're going to believe that."

"I can get you home." Trey followed her down the ladder. "Maybe they won't be up yet."

"No, we can't be seen together." Lila protested, yanking the car door open. "Just get me to town. Mrs. Melba saw you drop me off last night. I'll come up with a good story. They don't have to know we were together."

"Maybe they thought you went to bed and haven't woke up yet."

"Trey!" William's voice carried from the yard.

Lila dove onto the floorboard as Trey sat up in the driver's seat. "Hi, Mr. Barrie!"

"Good morning, Trey," William answered. "I wasn't sure you'd be awake. They're letting Dave out this morning. We're going to bring him to our house." He eyed the boy. "We're making you a bed, too."

Trey nodded. "Thanks, that sounds great. I'll see if I can get off work and meet you at the hospital this morning."

William nodded, hesitating. "You all right?"

"Fine." Trey smiled to show he meant it. "I have to go. I'm going to be late."

And there was a girl huddled on his floorboard.

# 11

W here are we?" Lila's hiss rose from the crevice in front of the passenger's seat.

"Main Street," Trey replied through a carefree smile.

"What time is it?" Lila asked.

"You don't want to know," Trey answered. "No more questions. People are watching, and I look like an idiot talking to myself."

He waved at another pedestrian before he turned onto Lila's street. In a few minutes, she'd be safely home with no one the wiser.

At least, she would be if Mrs. Melba wasn't watering the flowers in her front yard.

Trey gripped the steering wheel. "Mrs. Melba's out."

Lila growled. "Take the block."

Trey waved at the woman and turned the street corner. "Can you sneak in the back door?"

"No. It's always locked. Grandmother never uses it."

Trey pressed the gas, then the brake, trying to decide whether to speed up to get Lila home sooner or slow down to give Mrs. Melba plenty of time to finish drowning the flowers and go inside.

When he turned back onto Lila's street, he slowed. "She's

still out there."

"Drive slow and ask her if she knows if May has had her baby yet."

"What's that got to do with anything?"

"Mrs. Melba will get curious and go inside to find out."

It was worth a try. Lila had a knack for getting out of scrapes.

Trey slowed his car. "Hey, do you know if May had her baby yet?"

"Last night." The woman nodded matter-of-factly.

Oh. Great. Trey searched for another question. "At the hospital?"

"Yes."

"Is she still there?"

The woman dropped the hose to continue flooding the flower bed. Her chin jiggled as she hustled toward his car. "They said she was coming home this morning."

Trey tapped the gas, easing the vehicle forward. "Oh. Okay. I was just wondering. Thanks."

"Have you seen Lila?"

Trey stiffened. "Not since yesterday. Why?"

"She came home last night, but she was gone this morning when Mrs. Howard knocked on her door," Mrs. Melba said. "They were hoping she was with you."

They were *hoping* she was with him? Either her grandfather harbored a bit of bloodlust, or they expected to find Lila dead in a ditch somewhere.

Trey punched the accelerator. "I didn't know she was missing. I'll help look."

As soon as he turned the block, Lila squirmed to sit up on the floorboard. "You're a lousy liar."

"Well, what did you want me to say?" Trey asked. He palmed

the air in a mock conversation. "Don't worry about her, Mrs. Melba. She was sleeping with me all night."

Lila put her face in her hands and groaned.

Trey drove through the alley to park behind her house and killed the engine. "They know," he said.

Lila shoved herself onto the seat. "They're never going to believe the truth."

Trey shoved open his door, circling the car to open hers. He held out his hand. "Come on. I'll go with you."

"What are we going to tell them?" Lila spat.

"The truth."

Lila wrapped her arms around her stomach and moaned.

Trey tried again. "Come on. I promised if we were caught, I'd tell them it was my fault. You won't get into trouble."

She slit her eyes at him. "It's always the girl who gets into trouble."

Trey shrugged. "It's the best I can offer."

Lila swung her feet from the car and slid beside him, eyes leaking more than a little fear.

Trey's empty stomach churned as they neared the back door. As Lila warned, the door was locked, so he rapped on the wood. His fingers tightened around Lila's hand as footsteps inside sent the girl leaning back toward the steps.

Cool air hit his face as Lila's grandmother peered out, then threw open the screen. "Oh, thank God. Alex!" The woman pulled Lila inside. "Alex, she's here with Trey!"

Lila sputtered as the woman smothered her in a hug.

Reverend Howard strode in from the living room, huffing for breath. He eyed both teens.

Mrs. Howard grasped Lila's arms. "Honey, are you all right?"

"Yes," Lila answered, as though that should be obvious.

"Where have you been?"

Trey cleared his throat. "We didn't mean to stay out all night. We were talking, and we fell asleep."

Husband and wife exchanged glances before Reverend Howard's eyebrows drew. "I think you'd better come with me."

Trey had never been sent to the principal's office, but this felt much worse. He sent a look toward Lila, begging her to not make up any stories with her aunt as he followed the man. His hands retreated to his pockets before he forced them back out and his jitters traveled to his feet.

Reverend Howard sat on the couch, studying him before he asked, "Suppose you tell me where you and Lila were last night and what you were doing?"

"Um," Trey fumbled. Somewhere between the car and the house, his mouth had grown completely dry. He wondered if Melba was listening from behind a window screen.

The truth. He had to tell the truth like he'd promised Lila. "We didn't mean to stay out all night. We were at my house in the loft—just talking—and we fell asleep. Nothing else happened, I swear," he added as the reverend's eyebrows climbed to impressive heights.

The man tongued his teeth, weighing that information before he commented, "Must have been quite the discussion. What else were you doing all afternoon?"

He couldn't find any good way to j ustify stealing a work truck to sneak to a forbidden dance. Trey chewed his tongue, keeping his eyes on the man's forehead.

"We were dancing," he said. "I wanted a partner, so I offered to teach her. I talked her into going to a dance hall with me—so we went—but we didn't stay long, and we argued on the way back. I dropped her off here, but she came to my house to explain about the argument, and we were talking things out when we fell asleep. It wasn't intentional."

"And that's the truth?" the man asked.

"Yes, sir."

It was the first time that he was glad that his parents were dead, and Dave was confined to a wheelchair. His brother couldn't be much of a threat when it came to doling out punishment. However, no one could despise a reverend for handing out some sort of retribution.

Reverend Howard rubbed his chin for several seconds before asking, "How did your car end up abandoned on the road?"

"Oh." Trey squirmed. Sneaking off with a girl was one thing. Stealing a truck could land him in jail. "Um, my car ran out of gas, so we took Mr. Barrie's truck."

"And did Mr. Barrie know you were taking my granddaughter to a dance in his truck?"

"No, sir."

"Did he know you were taking it at all?"

"No, sir."

"So you stole Mr. Barrie's truck to take my granddaughter to a dance?"

It wasn't stealing. They were bringing it back. Trey nearly used the excuse that Lila had given him, but he swallowed it.

"Yes, sir."

Reverend Howard stopped asking questions.

Trey wished he was at the hospital visiting Dave instead of standing in a living room, pretending he wasn't about to wet himself. His hands won their war and crawled into his pockets, and his shoulders hunched like they were trying to follow.

Reverend Howard stood up, walking behind Trey to pick up the telephone.

Trey scrunched his eyes as Reverend Howard asked for Officer Morgan. Beams of sunlight highlighted an escape route leading to the front door, and it took every ounce of his self-control not to follow it. He stood motionless as the officer's voice scratched across the line.

"Hello, Morgan," Reverend Howard said. "Lila's home. She's safe. She's been with Trey. Yes, he's fine, too. No, I haven't seen any more of him. I don't think she does. If you find him, bring him in and I'll come down. I don't want him running off with her. Yes, sir. You too, sir."

The room swayed around Trey as Reverend Howard hung up the phone. "Thank you for telling me, Trey. We'll be talking more about this later. For now, I want you to figure out how you're going to explain to Mr. Barrie that you stole his truck."

Trey swallowed. "And Officer Morgan?"

"That's up to William." Trey felt Reverend Howard's eyes on the back of his head.

Trey swallowed. "Please, don't be mad at Lila. I talked her into it. It's my fault."

"Not really." The voice that spoke was so soft that Trey hardly recognized it as Lila's until she inched into the doorway. Her fingers interlaced an intricate pattern within each other. "Trey did ask me to dance, but I talked him into borrowing the truck." She stood tall under both men's stares. "He's also the one who wouldn't let me lie and said we should come in together."

For the first time, Reverend Howard was stunned into silence. He stared a full minute before the corner of his mouth perked in a smile.

Lila never saw it. Her eyes shifted to the window before she clamped her hand over her mouth. Trey followed her gaze, expecting to see Melba's nose over the sill.

Instead, he spied a man who stood on the road peering toward the house.

Lila gasped. "Dad!"

Reverend Howard caught her, swinging her away from the door. "No, Lila! No!"

"Let me go!" Lila fisted his chest, then screamed like she was being murdered. "Dad! *Vater!*"

Reverend Howard shoved her toward the back hall, shouting, "Trey, lock the door!"

Trey stayed rooted to the floor, unable to move as the door banged against the wall. The blond man filled the space in the door frame. Lila kicked her grandfather and rushed to wrap her arms around her father.

Reverend Howard sputtered and screamed, "Ralph, leave her alone! You cannot stay here! Lila, let him go."

Lila and her father ignored the orders. They clung to each other, speaking rapid German as her father tugged her from the door. Mrs. Howard's scream added to the chaos as she stumbled to the phone, yelling into the speaker to summon the sheriff.

Reverend Howard wrapped his arms around Lila's waist, wresting the girl away from her father. "Ralph, let her go! Lila's staying here."

Lila shoved against her grandfather, wriggling free before launching herself down the front steps with Ralph.

Trey jumped through the door and raced across the lawn to latch onto her hand. "Lila, no, don't go!"

A police siren sounded a few streets over.

Lila's eyes grew wide. She yanked her hand from his grip. "Trey, let me go! Don't stop me! I'll find you, I swear!"

Behind him, Officer Morgan's gun blasted from the end of the street.

Trey dove onto the ground, rolling before a tree trunk brought him to a stop. Lila screamed and her father dragged her between the houses, sending Mrs. Melba leaping into her flower bed. Trey ignored Officer Morgan's order to stay down as he launched onto his feet. He'd never catch up if he fell too far behind. He sprinted through the streets until he reached the woods, losing all glimpses of the pair.

His lungs burned as he gulped down air until a cramp in his side forced him to a stop. He was in the middle of a clearing with no idea which way to pursue them.

"Lila!"

Could she hear him?

"Lila!"

Did she even care?

—

Dave held his breath, resisting the urge to hiss as William helped transfer his weight onto the Barrie's couch. He had begged Laura to let him camp out in the living room instead of Luke's bedroom, claiming it would be easier for everyone if they didn't have to climb stairs.

Grateful the request had been granted, he complied as Laura hovered over him. When she covered his cast with a blanket, he thought that it would be just fine with him if neither he, nor anyone else, ever saw either leg again.

The farmhouse was clean, light, and cheery. Through the doorway to his side, Dave could see a sliver of Laura's kitchen. The window offered a view of the barn.

"Is it still aching?" Laura asked.

Dave nodded, but there wasn't much they could do about it.

Laura's hands went to her hips as she pressed her lips together in thought. "I wish we could find some way to make it stop."

"It needs time," William said.

Time. He'd be stranded on the Barries' couch for months. His body would shrivel even more than it already had.

Dave rubbed his face. "Where's Trey?"

"I'm not sure," William answered. "Maybe he couldn't get off work."

Dave took a breath, wondering how they were going to pay the hospital bills. He couldn't even work on the radios here. The screen door slammed, and the trio turned toward the entryway. Dave heard Trey's breathing before he spied the boy's swollen eyes.

"Where've you been?" he asked.

Trey's arms flailed limply. "He took Lila."

"Who?" Laura asked.

"Her father. He came and ran away with her. Reverend Howard called the police." Trey's breath huffed out. "They think he's a Nazi spy."

"A Nazi?" Laura wrung her apron.

"But he's not." Trey choked. "And they were shooting at them!"

"Trey." Dave cut his brother off, jutting his chin toward the porch as he spied Lila trudging down the end of the driveway with her slender arms wrapped around her waist. She was alone. She was safe.

Trey hit the screen door so hard that Dave winced and wondered if his brother would take it with him as he bolted across the yard. Lila clung to him, burying her face into his shoulder.

William opened the screen and waved the two kids inside. "Come in. Lila, are you all right?"

"Where's your dad?" Trey asked, though now he sounded more concerned over the man than angry with him.

"He's gone." Lila's throat worked. "He took a bus to Breeze City. I don't know where he'll go from there, but I told him not to come back."

"Oh, darling." Laura melted and mothered Lila into a chair. "Sit down. I'm sure we'll get everything sorted."

Lila rubbed her arm across her face. "I don't want to stay with my grandparents anymore. They'd just as soon have my father shot, and he's not a bad man. He's not."

Dave folded his arms. "Why didn't you go with him?"

Lila swallowed. She was a liar, Dave knew, and now he'd caught her. His eyes went to the window in case her father was lurking nearby.

"I decided not to," she said. "He can hide better without me."

Before Dave could press further, Trey sat next to Lila to take her hand.

"It's okay," he said. "You have a home here."

While William called Reverend Howard, Laura kept the teens busy in the kitchen, teaching them how to make cookies. Lila's face glowed with pleasure when she offered one to Dave, though her cheeks were still blotchy.

The smell and laughter reminded him of everything he'd spent the last few years trying to forget, and his mood darkened as the evening passed. He watched the others gathered around the table, feeling lonely on the couch and aching for his parents.

Lila looked nearly as miserable when William led her to the truck to take her home for the night. Laura settled Trey in Luke's room, wiping tears as she reached the bottom of the stairs. When the lights were turned off, the agony in Dave's leg invaded his thoughts, following him into a fitful sleep plagued with dreams.

Steel blue eyes zeroed on him. The man extended his arm, pressing a steel barrel into Dave's skull. "And now you die, soldier."

Twin gunshots blasted, their sounds intermingling from in

front and behind him. The soldier fell backward, crushing his skull against the street.

A faint American voice buzzed through the ringing in Dave's ears. "I've got you. Hold still. I'm getting you out."

His rescuer stepped around Dave, thrusting a broken beam into the rubble at Dave's knees. The movement spurted blood from the boy's arm, soaking his sleeve.

"Are you hit?" Dave asked.

"Yeah." The boy flashed blue eyes toward Dave, working a faint smile that didn't seem real. "Think they'll let us go home now?"

The feeble joke was lost in pain as the boy dropped his weight onto the beam, lifting some of the pressure that pinned Dave's legs to the ground.

*Home.*

Dave gritted his teeth, inching himself toward freedom. One leg shot pain while its counterpart dragged like a body bag.

A series of German commands echoed through the streets around them, growing louder as tanks rumbled.

Dave kicked with the only leg he could control, clutching at any firm handholds he could find. "Get me out! Get me out!"

The soldier abandoned the beam, using his hands to pull away the debris. From the corner of his eye, Dave spied the Nazi soldiers rounding the buildings at the end of the street. They were out of time. He'd be trapped and helpless while a German leveled a bullet at him. "Don't leave me!" He jerked against his constraints, feeling something tear through his leg. "Get me out!"

The boy wrapped his hands around Dave's arms, pulling until an involuntary scream ripped through Dave's throat. His companion gave a last tug, and he felt himself being dragged free of the concrete and steel. His mangled legs left a trail of blood, sending blinding pain through his body. He wished they'd just rip off and stay beneath the rubble.

A gun blasted, and the hands gripping his arms relaxed. His comrade crumpled, splaying his fingers across his collarbone. Blood spurted from his fingers. Dave jerked the gun from his companion's holster, turning a retaliation of bullets onto the murderer, screaming obscenities he didn't even fully understand. He couldn't carry his friend or even support himself, but he felled their enemy.

He swung his eyes toward the gasping boy. "Come on, Luke. Come on, we'll get sent home for sure now."

Hope lit Luke's eyes before they dulled and his head rolled back, leaving Dave the only one alive and screaming.

He was still screaming when he was shaken awake, waking to eyes similar to the dulled pair that haunted his dreams.

Moonlight highlighted the furrows in William's brow as he bent over Dave in the dark. "Are you all right, Dave?"

It took nearly three minutes to bring his breathing to a slow pace. Dave rubbed at his eyes as his mind sorted out the past from the present and dream from memory, feeling drowned in waves of guilt. "I'm sorry. I didn't mean to wake you."

William settled back with a shaky sigh, sitting for a moment longer before he said, "Dave, I know you don't want to think about it, but I want you to consider staying with us. You shouldn't be alone if Trey decides to go away to college."

*College.*

Jealousy panged. How different things might have been if he'd gone to college instead of war. He glanced toward William. For all of them.

He sucked in a breath. "I can't stay here."

William cocked his head. "Why, Dave?"

Dave's chest rose and fell. It was growing harder to keep

these secrets and live with their shame. His eyes fixed on the picture on the mantle. "Because it's Luke's house."

William stared softly. "Luke?"

Dave's hands trembled under the blankets, and he wished he was asleep right now. "I know what happened to him."

The silence hung in the air between them. He didn't dare look, but he heard William settle into the chair before he asked, "Oh?"

It was growing hard to breathe. Dave's eyes stayed on the window, watching stars twinkle and fade. "A Nazi was going to shoot me when I was trapped in the rubble. Luke shot him first. He was trying to dig me out when another guy shot him." His eyes squeezed together with the effort of telling. "I don't know what happened to his body or why he was never found. I don't remember. I just remember waking up in the hospital while they were stitching my legs back together."

The old man wiped his mouth, then his entire face. "I knew before we received the telegram that he had died."

"How?" Dave asked.

"I don't know exactly," William replied. "I woke one night and just knew. I didn't tell Laura. Even after the telegram came, and she kept hoping."

Guilt rippled through Dave's chest. "I should have told you before. I just couldn't think about it while I was healing. Then, I started to tell Lucy, and . . . she left." His words slowed as he continued. William had been a good neighbor and almost like a grandfather. Lucy was right that he deserved to know. And Dave couldn't die with the secret. "I wasn't fighting well that day. I was running away." He rubbed his face. "I knew if I obeyed orders, I would die, so I ran. I don't even know what I planned on doing. I just lost my head. If I hadn't been hiding in that building, it wouldn't have fallen on me."

Tears threatened to come now. He laid his fingers across his eyes, but William's hand touched his arm. "You got scared and ran. Everyone's done that sometime or another. Your moment just had bigger consequences."

Yes, it did. Luke was dead. He was crippled. His girlfriend knew he was a coward.

William took a deep breath. "Is this why you never go into town anymore?"

Dave swallowed and shrugged.

"What are we going to do about that?"

Dave shifted, rubbing a knot from his arm, feeling like he was a kid and his father was asking how a window had gotten broken.

William folded wrinkled hands. "You can't just spend the rest of your life hiding in a house. You've adjusted to your limits now. You can work on finding what you can do despite them."

"I can't dress myself in the morning," Dave growled. "I can't even fix the stupid radios. I don't know how."

"You can help me," William said. "Your hands are still good, even better than mine. There are plenty of things you can do here." He rose, brushing his sleeping pants like he was wiping off the past. "It's not up to us to question why one person dies and another lives. You lived. Don't waste your life wondering why. Nobody wants that. Not Luke. Not me, not Trey. You've suffered long enough. It's time to let it go."

The man's eyes filled as he offered a weak smile. Dave watched the wall long after the man left. By morning, he woke with a new sort of burden. He couldn't end his life now. But if he didn't end it, what could he do with it?

# 12

"V_ater?" The door squeaked as Lila opened it just enough to slip inside the barn. Hay rustled as she reached the last stall. Sandwiched between a musty horse blanket and the wall, Ralph looked even worse today than he had when she had left him. He had always been thin, but pain made him paler, creating a gauntness that couldn't be hidden by the stubble of his light beard.

He winced as he pulled his legs toward him. "Are the roads clear yet?" he asked.

Lila put her hand on his shoulder. "No. The entire town is talking about you. You'll have to hide a while longer." She dropped to her knees to rummage through her book bag. "I brought you something to eat. I'll bring more later when I can."

Ralph set his head against the wooden planks. "I will be all right."

Lila swallowed as her eyes fell to the threadbare laces and broken heel of the boot he'd set aside. He had walked a long way to come for her.

She swallowed, reverting to his native tongue. "How's the ankle? Do you think it's only sprained?"

Ralph shook his head, swallowing so hard she could see a

trace of his Adam's apple. "I think it's fractured. I can't stand on it at all."

Lila winced. They had depended on the river to be a friend to erase their tracks and scent. They hadn't counted on its treacherous rocks and strong current ripping a rotted boot.

She shifted to sit next to him. "You'll be safer here than anywhere else. Even if we snuck you out of town, you'll be no good if you can't walk. The Cunninghams are staying next door. Dave can't walk either, so he can't sneak up on you. I'll try to steer Trey from the barn. You should be left alone here."

Her father draped an arm around her shoulder, pulling her into his side. She felt his ribs through his shirt and swallowed.

Ralph searched her face before asking, "Are you happy here, Delilah?"

She felt tears spring, but anger released her breath. "Since when does it matter if I'm happy?"

"I thought if you were in the orphanage, you might have a chance to find a family."

Lila's eyes fell to her knees. "You are my family."

Her father shook his head. "As long as we are together, you will be in danger. I came only because I feared that your grandparents would hate you because they hate me."

"They aren't cruel to me. But they won't allow me to talk about you or even call me by my real name." Lila chewed her lip, peeling a splinter from her sock. "But I don't know if I want to leave."

She felt both his pain and his relief. "Then you are happy here?"

"I like Trey and the Barries. Even Dave," she answered. "The townspeople aren't very friendly, but I think they would be if I didn't lie so much. I've been dancing with Trey. He likes me." She shifted. "But I don't want to lose you either."

They sat in silence before he patted her leg. "I'm not going anywhere today. You should go to school. I'll be here when you come back."

Despite his reassurance, Lila hugged him tightly in case he was wrong. At school, she kept her eyes open and her mouth shut. Whispers faded when she walked into the room, but by the end of the day, she had heard half a dozen reports of where the German spy might be hiding and none of them were right.

After a week of no news, a local farmer's truck collided with a motorcycle and the gossip mill found fresh fuel. Lila spent her afternoons at the Barrie farm, where Laura taught her how to cook. William kept Dave busy mending small things. Trey bounced back and forth, lamenting each day on his way out the door to go to work.

Even Dave's temper softened. When Martha stopped by to see Laura and ended up talking more to Dave, the boy actually listened. The windowpane framed the unlikely couple as Trey and Lila peered from the swing.

Trey wrinkled his nose. "I don't see it. He doesn't look that interested."

"He's Dave," Lila argued. "He didn't even let her into the house before, remember?"

"He's not in our house anymore." Trey shrugged. "He can't order her to leave Mr. Barrie's farm. Only Mr. Barrie can, and he won't."

"I'll bet three dollars that they end up dating by the end of the year," Lila said.

Trey grinned. "You don't have three dollars."

Lila bit her lip. "Fine then. A kiss."

Trey's eyebrows perked, but for once, he played coy instead of falling for the first chance. "Not enough."

Lila pushed her lips to one side, feigning thought. "How about a three-minute kiss?"

"Deal."

"And your wager?"

Trey grinned. "The same."

Lila giggled, weaving her fingers in and out of his as she said, "So they're having the dance-off at the diner."

"Yep."

"We could win that, you know."

"Except you can't dance there," Trey reminded.

"I know." Lila shifted toward him. "I want you to talk to my grandfather."

Trey stared. "What difference is that going to make?"

"Perhaps none." She shrugged. "But you are the only person in the world who ever got me to stop lying. Besides, if we're going to dance there, we can't keep it a secret. We may as well try to get his permission."

"Lila asking permission?" Trey turned toward her with cocked eyebrows.

She shrugged lightly. "It's worth a try. It beats sitting out all night."

Except that Trey would have to go do the convincing. The man already didn't trust him, and there wasn't any reason why he would start now.

Trey swallowed. "I'll see what he says."

Lila smiled.

The next Sunday after he'd sweated through a sermon, he was less sure of success than he had been the night before. He blew out a breath, shifting his feet as he waited until the congregation emptied the sanctuary, though he had a sneaking suspicion that Lila would be listening from a crack somewhere.

Reverend Howard took his time closing the big Bible on the pulpit before he asked, "What can I do for you, Trey?"

Trey hesitated. He'd had an entire week to figure out what he was going to say, but all he could manage was to blurt, "I wanted to know why you don't want Lila dancing."

The man stared a moment before he took off his spectacles to rub his nose. "Why are you asking?"

"Well, we're having a dance-off at the diner. It's a fundraiser, and lots of adults are going to be there. I'd like to take her."

The reverend studied Trey before he huffed. "I appreciate you asking this time, Trey." That seemed to be the end of it, but the man stood a bit longer. "I will allow you to take her to this dance, but I'll be there to watch you."

Trey steadied himself on a pew before his body reeled with his mind. "Really?"

"Really."

Trey stopped himself before he started dancing in the sanctuary. "Thank you, sir. You're welcome to watch." It would be awkward, but at least it wouldn't be a secret.

Lila wasn't as discreet. As soon as Trey reached the bottom of the steps, she slung her arms around his neck. "Trey, you're amazing!"

Oh, yes. It was worth the sleepless night and the sweaty sermon. It was also worth the look on everyone's face when he walked into the diner with Lila on his arm. She had outdone herself wearing the same red polka-dotted dress she'd worn the first day they met, but she didn't look like the same girl.

Susan explained the rules for the fundraiser. "Your feet must be in motion for as long as you can last. Then you must sit until only one couple remains."

All proceeds went for new books for the library's tiny

collection. The mayor started the competition with a lively jitterbug. Trey smiled at Lila as he took her hand. They hit the floor at full speed, forgetting about their audience until the clapping made the transition to the second song.

Lila's feet froze for a split second before Trey swung her into the dance again. She spun toward him, then back, jutting her chin toward the door. "Look who's here!"

Trey glanced to the side to see two small wheels, followed by two large ones, roll over the threshold. Dave's face was clean-shaven, making him look more like the boy the town remembered, but the effect was countered by pale skin and trembling hands. William winked from behind Dave as he accompanied Laura.

Trey's grin grew even larger. He was dancing with the girl he liked without sneaking, and Dave had come to watch.

The third song followed the heels of the second, and Lila threw back her head in laughter. "This is harder than I thought. When are they going to play a slow one?"

They kept swinging, spinning, and sneaking glances at Reverend Howard, who seemed nearly as uncomfortable as Dave. Gradually, the reverend began to relax, and after the fourth song, he tapped his foot in the shadows of the table.

Dave watched the dancers, unsure if he would rather join them or leave. He swallowed jealousy as William slid a Coke float to him and jutted his chin toward the two kids.

"Something tells me they didn't start dancing together tonight," he said.

Laura giggled. "I would say not." She grabbed her husband's hand as the music turned to a slower tempo. "Oh. We can dance to this one. Come on. Go with me?"

William's eyebrows went up, teasing. "You think we'll survive in there?"

"I can." The woman's eyes rose imperiously. "I'm not sure about you, darling. We can sit out if you think you're too old."

Dave grinned.

William sighed, then glanced toward Dave. "Guard the floats, will you?"

"No problem," Dave answered.

William's eyes sparkled as he towed his wife to the edge of the dance floor. The younger people roared with encouragement and laughter as the pair shuffled and swayed like a couple who had been dancing together for a very long time.

Dave watched until a group of teens pressed so close that he struggled to breathe. They were laughing, jostling each other, and blocking him from the exit.

"Y'all behave over here."

Dave's hands froze against the wheels of his chair as the voice pierced his chest. Lucy wove through the teens, teasing until she spied him. She stopped, locking eyes with his in a cruel spell that neither of them wanted.

"Dave," she sputtered.

Dave's heart seared and softened at the same time.

Lucy's hands wrung each other as she swayed away, then back. "I didn't know you would be here."

Dave forced his fingers to unclench from his armrests. "I came for Trey."

"Oh." Lucy wet her lips, then said sincerely. "I'm glad. Trey's a very good dancer."

Almost as good as he had been. The words hung unspoken between them.

Dave cleared his throat. "Yes, he is."

Lucy tried to step away, but the teenagers were huddled together, whispering bets on the couples. Her hand flailed before she said, "I saw you let him have the car."

Dave glanced down at his fingers. She remembered that car too. The proposal. The backseat the night before he'd shipped out.

"Yeah," he whispered.

Lucy lowered herself onto a stool, crossing her ankles. She watched the dancers, ignoring him before she asked softly, "How are you?"

How was he? What was he supposed to say to that?

"I'm not very good."

Her shoulders fell. "Oh."

Dave sucked in a breath. "I hear you're having a little one."

"Yes. Sheldon's hoping it'll be a boy."

"And you want a girl?"

She closed her eyes before whispering, "I don't really care."

Dave glanced over, surprised. "If it's a boy or girl, or if it's born?"

Lucy pressed two fingers into her eyes. "You must think I'm a terrible person."

Dave shrugged. "We all have our faults." He was a coward, remember?

She gnawed at her lip. "It has nothing to do with the baby, really."

"Then what? You're not happy with Sheldon?"

"I didn't say that." Lucy's throat pumped, apparently unable to say anything else either. She stood, then paused without turning. "I'm sorry, Dave. I should have stayed."

Dave's hand flew to his head as the world dipped around him. By the time he'd found his balance, she was too far away to hear anything less than a shout. He watched the door jingle above the crowd and glimpsed her passing the window. Someone whispered something behind him.

Why had she said that unless she meant to torment him? She

was married. It was too late. Their chance was as shattered as the leg that kept him from kicking deep dents into his wheelchair.

He felt eyes on him and masked the turmoil. Before he'd found an escape route, Martha sank onto the stool beside him. "Dave, are you okay?"

No. He wasn't. Had she seen? Worse, had she heard?

Martha leaned forward. "You look like your legs are hurting."

Dave glanced sideways at her, sensing concern but not jealousy. He managed a nod. His legs were hurting, but not as much as his chest.

Martha motioned toward the door. "You want to go outside? Or will that make it worse?"

Dave eyed the door, imagining rolling over anyone who stood in his way. He had to get out. He pushed himself through the group, who cleared a path. Outside, he sucked in the cooler air as Martha walked beside him. Later, he might wonder what people said about their exit, but right now he didn't care about anything except easing the searing emotions.

Lucy. He couldn't decide if he wanted to rescue her and kiss her or pretend tonight never happened. Why was Martha even bothering to stay nearby?

Martha's voice broke softly into his thoughts. "What's the matter, Dave?"

Dave swallowed, fingering his chair. "I want to go home."

"You just got here." Her voice softened with disappointment. "Come on. It's not so bad. People will talk to you, I'm sure, when we go back in. You could have a lot of fun tonight."

Dave shook his head. "I don't want to see anyone."

Martha sighed and knelt in front of him. "Dave, you can't hide forever. Why do you make things so hard for yourself?" She touched his knee.

His torso jerked as he slapped her hand away. "Stop it!"

She fell backward, catching herself with a hand on the sidewalk and blinking in surprise. "Does that hurt you?"

"Don't touch my legs."

Martha shifted to her knees. "When are you going to understand, nobody in this town despises your legs as much as you do? They don't bother me at all."

Dave glared. "You can't see them."

"You're right. I can't." She reached again for his knee, whispering, "No one else can either."

Dave covered his face, letting out his breath. "Martha, you're wasting your time. You need somebody better than me."

Martha winced as a tiny sound escaped her throat. She looked at his shoes, then through the window of the diner. After a moment, she nodded. "Well. I have a lot of time to waste. I think you're worth it even if you don't."

"Why?" He stared. "You're a pretty girl and you're smart. You can find somebody. You just need to stop trying so hard."

Her fingers curled. "I did find somebody," she said. "I just can't make myself like anybody else. I never could, and honestly, if I can't have him, I'd rather have nobody." She took a breath, then nodded as she stood. "Good night, Dave."

—

Trey's feet throbbed with every step. He was developing a horrible gut feeling that Lila would outlast him. He glanced at the clock, where the large hand had already completed one circuit, then at the door where Dave had disappeared with Martha.

"They're not in yet," Lila said. "You owe me a kiss."

Trey grinned. "You don't know anything. You might be owing me one."

Lila's grandfather rested his chin in one hand, half asleep at the table. Laura and William were teasing each other by the looks of the woman's raised eyebrow. Laura never challenged William unless she was flirting.

Lila spun away, glancing toward the door as it jingled. The mayor moved to hold it for Dave as the boy wrestled to hold the door and wheel himself inside. He was alone.

"Shoot," Lila said.

Trey winced. Even with a promised three-minute first kiss, victory wasn't sweet. He frowned as Dave sent a half-hearted smile toward Laura as the couple moved to greet him.

"Dave!" A shout clashed against the music.

Trey and Lila jumped, breaking set as they swung toward the entrance. The bell on the door yelped as Sheldon's hands slammed against the glass. The smell of alcohol wafted through the air as he shoved into the building, stumbling through the crowd and whipping his head in every direction until he spied the wheelchair.

Dave backed his wheels toward the wall as the man surged forward. Sheldon grabbed Dave's arms, hauling him from his chair and shaking him like a dog.

"What did you do to her?" Sheldon shouted just as the song ended, bringing all festivities to a stunned silence.

Dave grabbed Sheldon's arms to keep from falling.

Trey sprang toward the pair, slamming into Sheldon's back. "Let him go!"

"Sheldon, stop it!" Lucy's scream covered Trey's command. The woman panted at the door, cradling her enlarged stomach.

Sheldon dropped Dave, then shoved Trey against the jukebox. He turned and slammed his foot into Dave's ribs.

"That's enough!" Mayor Taylor grabbed both of Sheldon's arms, pulling him toward the counter.

Sheldon strained against Mayor Taylor, lurching toward Lucy, shouting, "Should have married *him?*"

Every eye in the room fastened on Lucy. She covered her face, crying into her hands until Laura hurried over. The woman glared at Sheldon as she set her hands on Lucy's shoulders. "You ought to be ashamed of yourself! She's carrying your child."

Trey's insides curled as he ran to Dave, sliding on his knees across the floor. "Dave, are you all right?"

Dave's eyes were glazed with pain, but they swung past his former friend and melted on Lucy. The look lasted only a moment before Sheldon wrested away from the mayor.

Trey planted himself in front of Dave, shouting, "Don't touch him!"

William reached for Sheldon's arm. "Come on, son. You're drunk. Let's go talk somewhere else."

Sheldon shoved William into the stool near the bar. "Don't you know who that guy is?" He shot an accusing finger through Trey to Dave.

William sagged against the counter, sinking onto the stool as Sheldon continued his rant. "He's not a hero! He's not even a soldier!" Sheldon's arms flailed. "He's a deserter. He's a coward! He left his squad. He disobeyed orders and left! And then his legs were trapped and Luke . . ." Sheldon spun and pointed to Laura, who swayed against Lucy. "Your son—tried to dig him out until they blasted his chest open!"

Laura collapsed, and Lucy clung to her, trying to soften the woman's fall. Lila sprang to grab Laura's arms.

Lucy's eyes went to Sheldon as she yelled, "Sheldon, stop!"

Sheldon spewed spit as he shook his finger at her. "You married me! *Me!*"

Officer Morgan pushed his way through the crowd from the door, moving to handcuff Sheldon. "Come on, son. Let's go get you sober."

"Me? Arrest him!" Sheldon screamed as Morgan dragged him into the street. "He's the traitor! He doesn't deserve to live!"

"That's not true!" Trey yelled as the door barred Sheldon's shouts, leaving the room in a stunned quiet.

The mayor cleared his throat. "Ladies and gentleman, we have four couples still on the floor who will resume the competition next Saturday evening. Show's over for tonight. We're closing up."

William moved to guide Laura to sit at a booth. Lucy hunched over, leaning against the wall. Dave stayed on the floor with one elbow covering his face. The arm that he leaned on trembled so badly that it threatened to collapse beneath his weight.

Reverend Howard shooed the crowd toward the door, and the room began to empty. Trey saw the looks that Dave shielded himself from, the glances of pity and glares, and wondered the same thing they were. Was it true?

He gripped his brother's shoulder to whisper, "Dave?"

Laura gasped, pulling in a breath for the first time since Sheldon described Luke's death. William hugged her, smothering every long breath that covered whatever he was shakily whispering in her ear. Dave's hands shook as he moved them to his ears, clamping out the sound of the woman's sobs.

Trey felt Lila's arms slip around his shoulders as she knelt next to him. Even the reverend joined them on the ground, reaching to touch Dave.

"God is forgiving," the reverend said. "No matter what happened."

Trey choked. He'd scream that nothing had happened if Dave wasn't writhing in guilt.

"Mr. Barrie . . ." Lucy's voice rasped. She swayed before whispering, "I'm sorry. I'm so sorry."

For the first time in his life, William gave no response. He glanced at the girl, blinking a few times before dropping his face slowly back onto his wife's head.

Lucy squeezed her arms, turning toward Dave, but she swallowed her words and moved toward the door.

Dave's head lifted for the first time as she touched the door handle. "Lucy, stay."

She paused, leaning against the door.

"Please," Dave whispered.

Lucy swayed, squeezed her eyes tightly before she shook her head and choked, "I'm sorry, Dave."

The door jingled again as she left.

Reverend Howard stood. "Come with me, Lila. We need to make sure she gets home safely."

Lila squeezed Trey's shoulder before she rose. She touched Dave's head as she passed. Dave's hollow gaze moved from the empty doorway to the weeping woman near the counter. Trey tried to catch his eye, but Dave wilted, keeping his eyes on the floor.

"Dave." Trey reached to hold him up.

Dave's arms wrapped around him.

Trey shifted to hold his brother, whispering, "It's okay, Dave."

Dave's fingers dug into his arm as he murmured, "I didn't want you to know."

"It's okay," Trey repeated, refusing to replace the fantasies he'd had of his brother winning the war with the true images of him running away.

Laura pulled away from William to rub her hands down her wet face. She sniffed as she shuffled toward the boys. Trey offered her a hand as she lowered herself to the floor. The woman settled herself, then reached for Dave's shoulder.

He crumpled beneath her touch, repeating, "I'm sorry . . . I'm sorry . . ."

Laura's hands wrinkled as she rubbed his shoulder. "Luke was not my only son." She glanced toward Trey, then back to Dave. "I still have two boys that I love just as much."

Dave gave the slightest of nods, giving no protest or eye contact, even when they finally settled him back onto the couch in the Barries' living room.

Laura announced that she was putting on hot chocolate for everybody. She smiled, striving for some semblance of normalcy, but her hands trembled and she dropped the pot before she even got the water to the stove. Abandoning the task, she disappeared to the bedroom.

Trey knelt beside the couch, avoiding the portrait of the soldier on the mantel. He squeezed Dave's arm softly as though the movement would access the part of Dave's brain where words currently had little effect.

"I don't care," he said. "Whatever happened, I don't care. Dave, please." Trey almost whined the name, desperate for some sign that Dave would eventually turn back to his normal, grumpy self.

Dave's breath leaked softly. "I'm fine," he whispered.

But he wasn't fine. His spirit—the part that made him Dave—withered. Nothing Trey said or did could bring it back.

# 13

Dave's leg throbbed when he woke, and each clang in the kitchen sounded like a train wreck. He wanted to be home. He wanted to be drunk. Honestly, he wanted to be dead. Laura's soft singing contrasted with his mood, and he mused how he might enjoy life here with this couple if he wasn't responsible for their son's death.

He wanted to go to the fields with Trey, trooping out behind William like faithful puppies. Laura's graciousness was felt so deeply that Dave wasn't sure how to process it. If he was going to stay, he had to find some way to make himself useful. He racked his mind, but his childhood at the dance studio and youth bent over the hood of a car hadn't prepared him for life without mobility.

The guilt and anger only further warped the depression until he stared dully at the wall. Laura didn't know that he was awake, but he wasn't ready for questions and mothering. He shrank into the cushions as someone knocked on the back door.

Laura shuffled across the wooden floor before the screen door creaked. "Why, Melba," she said. "I haven't seen you out here in a long time."

"I came to see how you were doing." Melba's voice oozed with concern. "I couldn't believe what happened last night.

Sheldon's still at the station now, but he's getting out at noon."

"I supposed he would," Laura answered calmly.

"How are you doing?"

"We're fine. Trey's out with William, and Dave's resting in the living room. He didn't sleep well."

Neither had Laura. Dave had listened to her crying in the bedroom at midnight.

"Mr. McGee has an extra room now that Peter's gone off to college. The boys could stay there with him."

Laura's voice grew frigid as she answered, "I've gotten used to having them here. I'd miss them if they went anywhere else. There's no reason why they—"

"Laura, I know you're a good Christian woman, and you and Mr. Barrie both have hearts of gold, but you're not really thinking things out. Trey will be off to college soon, and Dave can't stay alone at their home. They're about to foreclose on it anyway."

Laura's breath escaped in sync with Dave's stifled gasp. "Oh, Melba. Where did you hear that?"

"From my brother. Dave hasn't told you? He hasn't made their full payments in months, and Mr. Martin just can't do business like that. He's put it off as long as he can, but everybody knows that Dave's condition is permanent. There is nothing that he could do with that big old farm anyway. He can't even take care of himself."

Laura's heels became staccato, though her voice stayed low. "Well, I hope you'll convince Mr. Martin to reconsider, at least for a while. A farm means a lot to a man, and it is all those boys have right now."

"Honestly, Laura," Melba plowed forward. "I think going to live with Mr. McGee would be the best thing that ever happened to Dave. He wouldn't let him lie around all day. He would be sure he kept busy and useful. A body needs to be useful."

"He can be useful here," Laura's voice clipped her words.

Melba huffed. "I'm just going to come out and say it. You and Mr. Barrie aren't getting any younger and, no matter if it was an accident, having Dave around can't be good for your health now that you know about Luke."

Dave shook his head, though there was no one to see it.

"Melba." He could almost hear Laura's hands on her hips just through her tone. "You need to go home. Dave and Trey are staying with us, and that's all there is to it. I've lost Luke. I've lost four babies. I won't lose those boys, too. I won't do it."

"And just how do you think that Luke would feel about that?"

"Out!" Laura snapped. "Out! You are no longer welcome in my home!"

Melba huffed. "Well, Dave is no longer welcome in this town. He's not the only boy who went through hell in that war. He's got no excuse for keeping that kind of secret."

The door slammed, though it was difficult to tell which woman did the slamming.

Laura's breath came in shaky and deep before she crept to the living room doorway. Dave closed his eyes, trying to keep his own breathing calm and slow, feigning sleep. After a short battle of wills, where she waited for a sign that he had heard and he remained determined not to let her know, Laura shuffled back into the kitchen and busied herself with lunch, but her singing had been replaced by sniffles.

Dave scrunched his eyes. He'd find a way to make it right. He could earn his keep. But what about the townspeople? Though Laura and William's support was deeply felt, he couldn't let them annihilate themselves on his account. What happened when they couldn't afford their own farm? What happened if one of them died? When both of them went? He'd be helpless with no place to go and dependent on people's pity and kindness. Even if he found a job in the town, money wouldn't lift him out of bed in the morning.

He pressed his fingers against tears, almost glad that his parents had died and weren't witnesses to his shame. How would the people of the town react to Trey now? Had he ruined things for him as well? Did the entire town agree with Mrs. Melba? Were they right? How could a crippled man redeem himself for betraying his country and causing the death of an innocent boy?

He couldn't.

Dave sagged deeper into the couch, cussing under his breath. He was going to lose his home. The idea of a man hammering a foreclosure sign to his parents' yard seemed to sum up his existence.

When Laura went to the garden, Dave struggled to sit up. He had to get up. He had to find something—anything—to salvage himself. He tugged his chair closer to the couch and worked his way into it, refusing to call an elderly woman to help him.

He rolled to the doorway and down the board William had laid for a ramp the night before. It wasn't exactly a smooth ride or a painless one. Dave's chair lurched and threatened to topple, reminding him of the rush to get to the boys who forced peppers down his brother's throat. Was that his fault, too? He didn't know. He didn't even know exactly what he would do when he got home. He just needed to be there.

He was gasping for breath by the time he coasted into his driveway. His house sagged beneath the peeling paint. The ramp was too steep, and his heart lurched at the idea of tumbling off the porch again. Dave growled softly, mentally circling the house, but there wasn't any way to get inside. Stupid idiot. Why was he even here?

Jerking movements threatened to tangle his fingers into his wheels as he vaulted himself toward the barn where his car had sat for so long before Trey took ownership. Dave swallowed. Soon that car might be all they had left if the bank didn't snatch that up, too. He needed to get it in Trey's name before they had the chance. He should have warned Trey about the finances. He just didn't want the boy to feel any more pressure over money.

The barn was empty, and Dave coasted to a stop. He wasn't sure what he was looking for, but he wouldn't find any good solutions because there weren't any.

Melba was right. No matter what he did with the rest of his life, he was going to be a burden to somebody. He lifted his head toward the rafters, as if God lived up there and could give him answers. Was there something he could sell that could pay off the house for just a little longer? Could he sell that ring and buy a bit more time for Trey?

But it still wouldn't be enough, and that wouldn't solve the future problems. Before his thoughts could spiral downward, he spied the rafter again. The gun was inside, protected by the ramp, but there was a rope in the barn. His teeth grit. All the fantasies he'd had about sacrificing himself so that Trey wouldn't feel bound to him vanished. They'd just see him as a coward who ran away a second time, but what was his choice? Trey would hate him for a while and Laura might cry, but they'd be free of obligation to care for him.

Dave grabbed the rope, gathering its splintery lengths into his hands. This would be harder than pulling a trigger. He tossed the end toward the lowest rafter, watching it fall short and flop back to the floor. Who was he kidding? God was punishing him, condemning him to life.

Something shifted in the barn, raising the hair on his arms. Dave twisted in the chair, spinning it in a slow circle. He dropped the rope, getting rid of any evidence of a troubled mind before William stepped into the barn and gave him a heartfelt but worthless pep talk.

"Who's there?" he barked.

He rolled backward, reaching for a rusted pitchfork. Even with the silence, he felt the presence in the stable. His grip tightened as he tugged open a stall door.

A man stumbled to his feet, leaning heavily against the far corner. Dave stared at the pair of eyes so similar to the soldier that had ended Luke's life.

"You're the German," Dave sputtered.

The man's hands lifted, though they trembled slightly. He answered in broken English. "I am from Germany, yes, but I have not lived there in many years."

Somewhere in his mind, Luke's killer sneered. Splinters dug into his hands as Dave tightened his grip on the pitchfork.

The man sank to the ground. "I'm not here to hurt you. I only needed a place to stay. I came for my girl. My little girl, Delilah. You know her."

Lila's father. Dave trembled. He couldn't kill Lila's father, but hate still pulsated his fingers. "You left Lila once."

The man nodded. "I know. Soon, she will be on her own, and I will have to keep away again. But it is a hard thing to give up the only thing you have, is it not?"

"Why are you still here?" Dave asked. "Why not take Lila and go?"

"Winter is coming, and I have no home for her."

So he planned on living in the barn until spring? Dave eyed

the man until his attention snagged on the makeshift splint the man tried to hide.

"What happened to your ankle?" Dave asked.

The man's eyes roved, either making up a story or reviewing his options. Finally, he stuttered. "It . . . it was fractured when we were running. I underestimated . . . I tried to walk too soon." He motioned toward it. "Lila said no one would find me here, to hide while it heals."

Lila was wrong. Dave had found him, and though he was crippled, this man was nearly immobile. Images of lying on the street, looking up at someone who toyed with his life played through Dave's mind, and he felt a certain base pleasure in turning the tables. He could end this man's life. He could make him beg for it. Or he could turn him in, spare the man's life, and redeem his own reputation. Someone would come to the farm soon. He could hold him until they arrived. He could be a hero.

Ralph eyed him, repeating feebly. "I am not a Nazi. I only wanted a simple life. To work hard, marry, and raise a family. That is all."

"That's all anyone wants!" Dave snapped. "That's all I wanted! I had to go all the way across seas to put an end to your people's senseless killing, and now I won't ever get that."

Ralph took a breath, weighing his response. Finally, he said, "Then we are both miserable. But why should you do the thing you so despise?"

"I'm not going to kill you." Dave's voice dropped. "And if I do, it will be your fault. Someone will come soon, and I'll turn you in."

The man's face did not change, but his eyes ached. His mouth quivered as he spoke. "Why should you care if I live or die when you plan on dying yourself?"

"I'm not dying, and I won't die!" Dave snapped. "You'll go to jail, and I'll stay here and—"

And what? The question that he had forgotten returned with a vengeance.

"It's your fault!" Dave hissed. "It's your fault they hate me!" He drew back the pitchfork, hurtling it toward the man. Before he released it, he changed his aim, clattering the tool next to Ralph's head.

Nazi or no, he couldn't kill Lila's father. He backed his wheels to clear the stall. "Just leave my barn before they find you and blame me."

Ralph blinked rapidly before nodding. He gritted his teeth, gripping the stable wall as he shifted his weight onto his bad ankle. His pale face grew a shade lighter.

Dave turned his back, rolling to his father's toolbox. He rummaged through, running his finger over the hammer they'd used to build the tree house together, sensing the man linger behind him.

After a moment of busying himself with tools he had no use for, he growled, "Why are you still here? I can't help you walk."

"I fear to leave you alone," the man said softly.

"I live here," Dave answered. "I'm alone all the time."

"But you are troubled."

Troubled enough to hurl a few tools at the person who reminded him of the fact. Dave whirled his chair. "Why should you care if I'm alone or not?"

"Because," the man replied, "Lila told me about you. We are not very different, you know."

"I'm not a refugee quite yet," Dave growled. "You are, and if they come soon, they'll arrest you and probably me too." His voice rose as if he was yelling at a dog. "So get! Get out!"

Tires crunched as a car swung into the driveway, blocking

the refugee's retreat. The two men exchanged panicked glances.

"Dave!" Trey's voice barely preceded him before the boy rushed into the barn. "Dave, what—"

Trey skidded into the doorway, face contorting in surprise when he saw Ralph. Lila followed on his heels, sharing none of the shock that Trey expressed. Little deceiver, what had she been thinking to hide the man here?

She swung toward Dave, pleading, "He's my father."

"I know. Get him out."

Lila turned tearful eyes toward the ceiling. "He doesn't have anywhere to go. He can't walk yet."

"He can't stay here!" Dave yelled. "They're foreclosing the house! People are coming here this morning."

Ralph swallowed again, swaying on the injured limb. His breath shook as he ran fingers through his hair.

Lila took his arm. "We'll get you to the woods, so they don't find you. Then we'll find somewhere else for you to go."

"Delilah." Ralph took her arm but pushed her away instead of accepting the help. "Let me go by myself. They should not find you with me. Go back to your grandfather's."

"I'm not leaving you!" Lila snapped.

"I cannot walk far. They cannot find you with me. You need to make a home here."

The argument began in English but escalated into German, triggering memories that made Dave grip his armrests.

Dave's eyes swung to his watch, then back to the man and his tearful daughter.

"Trey, do you have the car keys?" he asked.

Trey dug them from his pocket. "Yeah. Why?"

Dave took the keys from Trey and tossed them toward Ralph. "Use your good foot. You can catch the train in Breeze City. We'll get the car later."

Surprise flickered across every face as the German caught the key chain.

Lila was the first to recover, whispering, "Oh, Dave." She took two steps toward the man in the wheelchair, throwing her arms around him and planting a kiss squarely on his cheek. "Thank you." Then she turned and gave quite another sort of kiss to Trey. A long, slow one that made the boy freeze, then grow limp.

Just as quickly, the girl spun away, taking her father's arm to help him hop to the car. As it roared to life, she turned to find Trey's eyes. "I have to go with him."

Trey stood stunned as Lila ran around the car, swinging into the passenger's seat as the man backed out.

"Wait." Trey stumbled forward as the car turned around. "Are you coming back? Lila?"

Lila gave no answer.

Trey stared until the car turned onto the main road. Then he spun and kicked the wheel to Dave's chair. "What was that? What are you going to tell them if they catch them in our car?"

"I'll tell them it was me. You play dumb."

"No!" Trey paced back and forth. "You shouldn't have let him go! She would have stayed."

"She would have hated you."

"If they're caught, you'll both be arrested!"

Dave swallowed, holding out an arm. "Come here."

Trey's breath escaped in a growl, but he moved into the embrace.

Dave fought for eye contact with the boy. "Lila needs her father free." Maybe the man was a Nazi. Maybe he had been lying. Lord knew Lila could. Or maybe the man really was a simple immigrant.

Trey jerked away. "Well, I hope you're happy. If they escape, I'll lose her, and if they're caught, I'll lose you."

A second car door slammed, and William's voice carried across the barnyard. "Trey? Dave?"

Trey folded his arms, but the tremor in his jaw betrayed his fight for composure. He turned and brushed past William as the man stepped into the doorway.

"Trey, what's the matter?" William asked.

Trey shook his head, refusing to answer. Dave's eyes averted as the man glanced around the barn, then toward him. "Dave? Where's Lila?"

Dave sucked in a breath. "Lila's father was here. I let him take the car, and she went with him."

William nodded softly. "I thought she was hiding him here. Lila kept walking this direction when you boys were at my house." He took off his derby to scratch the back of his head. "It's a hard thing when your family is on the line."

Engines buzzed outside, sounding like an entire fleet of cars were invading the driveway. Dave's eyes went back to the barn as fear gripped his chest. "You'll take care of Trey?" he asked suddenly. "If they arrest me?"

"Dave." William's voice carried surprised and pain.

"They might if they find him."

He heard a series of car doors slam. Had the entire town come out?

Martha's voice carried across the yard. "Mr. Martin, wait!"

Something in Dave's chest sliced as Melba called out, "Martha. Honey, what are you doing out here?"

Martha gasped for breath as if she had run the entire way there. "You're not really foreclosing, are you?"

"Yes, we are," Mr. Martin said.

"But it's Dave's house!"

"We've given him as much time as we can afford. He put the mortgage on it. He can't pay it off, and that's not going to change."

"Well, how much does he owe?" Martha asked.

"We can't tell you that," Mr. Martin insisted. "Go home, Martha. There's nothing you can do here."

"Could I buy it?"

Mrs. Melba laughed. "Honey, you couldn't afford this old dump. What would you do with it anyway?"

"I work," Martha argued. "I have savings."

Martha could be a determined little thing when she wanted to be, but Dave wasn't comforted by the idea of the farm going to her, any more than he was thinking about it going to the bank.

"I know you work. I know how much you charge, how many students you have, and how long you've taught," Mr. Martin said. "You don't have enough money for this house."

Apparently, it was true, because Martha fell silent.

Mr. Martin called out, "Trey, where's your brother?"

"He's in the barn." Trey's sullen answer came after a moment.

Someone gasped, but Dave couldn't tell who. His face pricked as the trio found him. Mr. Martin's spectacles perched high on his beaked nose as he led his sister through the wide doors.

Martha followed, hovering by the doorway, looking very close to tears herself. Mrs. Melba pressed her lips together, folding her arms with the sort of look that a teacher wore when chastising a favorite student.

Mr. Martin cleared his throat as he shoved a pile of papers toward Dave. "Son, we're going to have to foreclose on your farm. We need you to sign these."

William's hand landed on Dave's shoulder to steady him as

the words swam in front of his eyes. His father's farm. Trey's home. He needed more time.

"The two lines. Here and here." Mr. Martin pointed them out as though Dave were a child and didn't know what he was supposed to be doing. The pen was forced into limp fingers.

Please, don't . . . The words formed in his head, but his tongue was too weak to speak them. Dave's eyes flickered to the dusty rope, lying camouflaged among the tools.

"Dave, we don't have all day. Just sign the papers." Mr. Martin tapped his fingers against his arm.

A hammer pounded in sync with Dave's heart as someone drove a sign into the front yard. Dave's chest heaved several times as William's grip tightened on his shoulder. A tear dropped onto the page.

Martha lowered herself onto the platform that Dave had used to help Trey work on the car. "This is wrong," she muttered.

Dave scratched his name on the printed line.

*David Cunningham.*

"Good. Now sign here."

Was this because of Luke? Dave took a breath and signed.

Mr. Martin took the papers and pen, saying "good boy" as though Dave was a dog that had been taught to sit and stay.

Dave let his eyes close as the man walked from the barn. He covered his face with his hands as his shoulders shook themselves free of William's grasp. He was making a fool of himself, but the harder he tried to hold back, the louder he cried.

"Oh, Dave." Martha's voice came close, and her hand landed on his knee. She knelt in front of him, rubbing his leg. "You could—you could start over." She sounded like his mother. "You won't be alone." Now she sounded like she was trying to convince herself. "The Barries want you with them. If you don't want to stay there, you can come live with me. We don't even have to get married. I don't care what they say! I won't let you be alone. We could find something for you to do. I could teach you piano, and then you could teach, too."

Martha's hand dropped as her voice trailed away, and Dave heard Trey's shoes on the wooden floor. Dave forced a wet face up to his brother. Trey didn't look angry or accusing. He looked confused.

"Dave?" he asked.

Dave turned his face from both of them. "I'm sorry, Trey."

The pain numbed into a stupor as the hours passed. Martha left to help Laura ready their house for the boys. Trey hovered near the windows, peering bleakly at the fields. Instead of packing his things, he rummaged through the house until he found a candle. He lit it, placed it in his window, and amused himself with the melted wax.

Dave said nothing. At this point, Trey could burn the house down for all he cared. William stayed, asking questions Dave didn't want to answer.

"What else can you think of that you want?" William asked.

Dave swallowed. "It doesn't matter."

"It will later," William said.

Dave's eyes floated to his high school ring that had spent more time around Lucy's neck than on his finger. "Not once they find Lila is gone."

"He's her father," William said stubbornly. "Legally, he's still her guardian."

"Trey's never going to forgive me."

"He needs time," William said.

Time was all that Dave had left, yet it seemed the hardest thing to grant his brother. He folded a shirt and set it into a suitcase.

The hum of an engine caused both men to exchange glances as Trey called out, "Lila's back!"

Dave never thought he'd be glad to hear that someone was coming up the drive. He almost grinned as he wheeled himself into the living room to watch Lila carefully bringing the car to a stop with the pale face of a girl who was learning to drive. She stared at the window until Trey jerked open her door. Lila climbed out and tiptoed to hug him.

"Oh, boy." William chuckled.

Dave almost smirked. Trey was growing up and leaving them all behind, and there wasn't much that anyone could say about it.

Trey was useless after Lila arrived, and it was all Dave could do to get him to load up the boxes. Neither looked back as they pulled away from the house. Laura and Martha had emptied a downstairs room for Dave, giving him a place of his own away from Luke's old bedroom.

Laura insisted on unpacking his things, and the room began to look a bit familiar before night came. Dave wasn't in a chatting mood, but he didn't protest when Laura brought in her mending to keep him company when he was settled into the bed.

He heard Lila laugh as the porch swing creaked.

Laura smiled over the shirt that she was mending for Trey. "They're getting quite close, aren't they?"

Dave shook his head. "I don't know what we're going to do with them."

Laura bit the thread before she answered sagely, "Keep them within sight." Her chuckle faded as she studied him. "Dave? Why don't you date Martha?"

Dave squirmed. "Martha?"

Laura folded the shirt slowly. "I know she's probably not quite what you had in mind, but she's a sweet girl, and she really likes you."

Dave shifted. "Yeah. Luke liked Martha, too."

"Oh, I know." Laura sighed. "Luke liked her a lot more than she liked him. Every time I heard her talking to him, she was talking about you." She wrapped the thread around the button and shook out the shirt. "I think somewhere deep down she's hurting just as badly as you are."

"I doubt it."

"Well, at least say 'hello' tomorrow at the dance. You can do that much."

Dave swallowed. "I'm not going."

"You should." Laura set the shirt on the side table. "The longer you wait to go into town, the harder it will be."

Dave fingered his eyes, turning his face toward the back of the couch.

Laura reached over to trace his hairline. "You need to go for Trey. If no one else, he'll remember it. He's going to win tomorrow. You know he will."

Dave huffed a small laugh. "Yeah. I know."

"So you'll go for Trey and say hello to Martha while you're there," Laura said. She stood and smoothed out her skirt as if it was a done deal.

Dave fought a smile. "You're persistent."

Laura giggled. "Only when I need to be."

His emotions were spent, but he rubbed his head as he whispered, "I'll try."

"Good." Laura gathered up her sewing and pressed her lips lightly against his head. "Good night, son."

# 14

You know, if we were smart, we'd be saving our energy for the competition." The voice of logic sounded strange coming from Lila's lips.

Trey grinned, squeezing her hand as he pulled down the sidewalk past a row of abandoned buildings. "Since when have we been smart?"

"Since we have a competition to win in one hour," Lila reminded him, though she kept his pace, peering at their surroundings.

Trey ducked into the alley near a brick building, choosing the window with the least number of boards nailed across. He tugged the lumber until he found the few that were loose and pried them from the opening.

"Come on. It's the only way in."

Interest piqued, Lila bent next to him to grab the next board. "Why are we sneaking in here?"

"Because I want to show you something."

"My, my. He's so secretive," Lila teased. "It must be big for Trey Cunningham to break into a public building."

"Whose name was on that sign in front?" Trey asked casually, then smirked as Lila scampered around the corner to investigate the answer.

The last board loosened, clanging to the sidewalk, but the clatter didn't quite cover Lila's shriek. The girl returned, excitement animating her features. "Trey Cunningham, you did not tell me that your parents owned a dance studio!"

Trey stepped back to answer, but before he got a chance, Lila slithered through the window. By the time he navigated the narrow passage, the girl had circled the room twice. He brushed his hands on his jeans, unexpectedly confronted by memories of his parents. For the first time since they had died, he felt they could see who he had become and might even be pleased.

Lila's shoes echoed as she stepped around the scattered bits of the fallen ceiling. She fingered the faded curtains with the same pleasure of most girls discovering a new pair of shoes.

"This is incredible," she said.

Trey planted his hands on her shoulder to steer her toward the center of the room. "Now, imagine that the ceiling is repaired and the floors are swept."

Lila giggled as she twirled slowly. "And there are red velvet drapes cascading down the windows." She glanced at the fans with their globed fixtures. "And a chandelier."

Trey laughed. "How about two chandeliers?"

"And gold trimming around the walls." Lila's hand traced the path as though the material would appear in its wake.

Trey stepped behind her, putting his hands on her waist. "And you and I are teaching."

Lila smirked. "With Dave handling the paperwork, since everyone knows we couldn't."

They stood, lost in the daydream they had constructed together.

Lila turned to face him, hopeful trepidation showing in her eyes. "Do you think that we could really do it?"

"I hope so." Trey tugged her closer, slipping his hands onto her waist. "Because I'm going to buy it someday, and then I'm going to marry you in it."

Lila's eyebrows flew up in surprise. "Are you now?"

He gave her a lopsided smile. "I'm planning on it. What do you think?"

Lila's hands traced his shoulders as her eyes flickered in contemplation. "I think it's a good plan. All of it." She pressed her lips together and walked her fingers up his arm. "By the way. Remember that bet we made? Somebody owes somebody a kiss."

Trey's heart slammed as he wrapped his hands around her waist. "But who?"

"I guess we'll find out tonight." Lila grinned as she stepped back. "Prepare to lose. Now, come on. We've got a competition to win."

Trey reached for her hand, but the girl raced back to the hole in the window. As they slid through the gap to run down the road, their laughter echoed through the room and created the first sound of its future.

# About the Author

Lindsey Renée Backen finds inspiration in history, music, and acting. Living on the Texas coast, she works as a novelist, publisher, and local playwrite bringing her stories to life on both page and the stage. She is the author of *Swing, Across the Distance* and the *Between* Series.

To find more books by Lindsey,
please visit www.everinkpress.com.